A MAN: KLAUS KLUMP

A MAN: KLAUS KLUMP

GONÇALO M. TAVARES

TRANSLATED BY RHETT MCNEIL

DALKEY ARCHIVE PRESS
Champaign / London / Dublin

Originally published in Portuguese as *Um Homem: Klaus Klump* by Editorial Caminho, Lisboa, 2003

Copyright ©2003 by Gonçalo M. Tavares
Translation ©2013 by Rhett McNeil

First edition, 2014

Library of Congress Cataloging-in-Publication Data
Tavares, Gonçalo M., 1970-
    [Homem. English]
    A man : Klaus Klump / Gonçalo M. Tavares ;
    Translated by Rhett McNeil. -- First Edition.
       pages cm.
    "Originally published in Portuguese as Um Homem: Klaus Klump
    by Editorial Caminho, Lisboa, 2003."
    ISBN 978-1-62897-034-0 (pbk. : alk. paper)
    I. McNeil, Rhett, translator. II. Title.
    PQ9282.A89H6613 2014
    869.3'42--dc23
                          2014001185

This publication was partially supported by the Illinois Arts Council, a state agency and the University of Illinois (Urbana-Champaign).

Funded by The General Directorate for Book and Libraries — Direcção-Geral do Livro e das Bibliotecas / Portugal

www.dalkeyarchive.com

Cover: design and composition by Mikhail Iliatov
Printed on permanent/durable and acid-free paper

Nothing new. Money wasn't invented
Out of thin air: it was created in factories,
In thick chambers, in grand buildings.
In the city the taste of milk now calls machines to mind
More than cows. It's growing late, and the socks
                                    that were white
In the morning are black as they're pulled off at home.
The low-hanging smoke leisurely eats the busy
Ankles. The city is drinking wine, and some distracted
Parents are singing pornographic songs
To lull their children to sleep. If a person were to hear
                                    a cock crow
She would immediately think that the catastrophe
                                    has begun.

———————————————

—from *A Voyage to India*

A MAN: KLAUS KLUMP

PART I

Chapter I

1

A country's flag is a helicopter; gasoline is necessary to keep the flag aloft; the flag isn't made of fabric, but of metal; it waves less out in the wind, facing nature.

Let's move on to geography, we're still in a place that precedes geography, in the pre-geographic period. After History there is no more geography.

The country is unfinished, like a sculpture. Look at its geography: it lacks terrain, this unfinished sculpture. The neighboring country invades to complete the sculpture: warrior-sculptors.

Massacre as seen from above: sculpture. Bodily remains could be the beginning of other projects.

With some effort, a dog was plucked from the soil. Not a small tree, but a dog.

Animals don't resist like the botanical world, or like a hat. Hats get blown away by the wind, but dogs don't and trees never do. But sometimes a commotion comes through and nature shows off one of its splendors: evil. Hats, dogs, and even trees are all blown away.

Johana left the funeral home and went into a bar where men were stupidly singing the national anthem because there was an important game on. She lowered her eyes and asked for a glass of wine. We don't serve wine to women, said the man rudely; Don't interrupt men when they're singing the anthem. Johana had a stone in her pocket, a forceful stone; you could tell it was a forceful stone, small but dense; there is energy in things, a violent energy that the eyes can detect; Johana took the stone from her pocket and set it on top of the counter. This isn't a lamp, she said. If it turns on, it'll blind you. But she didn't say that, she thought it. The man understood. He said: If you want wine, I'll give it to you. He went in search of a glass, filled it with wine.

A starving machine. Johana stands up and spits on the machine. You put coins in it to listen to music, you don't spit. Coins, not spit, you see?

Johana goes to pay and argues about the price: It's too much, she says. It's a glass of wine, said the man, I'll just let you have it. Don't come back here again.

The man was smoking a cigarette, he was handsome, young. Johana looked at him and left. But she hadn't managed to leave even after she'd walked a hundred meters from the door, because she was still looking at him.

Tanks were entering the city. Military sounds entered the city, and serene music went into hiding throughout the city. Someone out in the street was wildly attempting to sell newspapers. Tanks were coming into the city, the news rushed into the paper.

But that doesn't happen; eyes were rushing over the news, people were uneasy; women weren't dying, but they could hear people dying.

Johana wets her pants.

I wet my pants, she says. Excuse me.

(The man beside her is not her brother.)

An extraordinary woman stares at an ant for a long time. Yes, an ant. A stupid, black thing. A black and holy land that advances along the world of the minuscule, down below our feet even, there are things that are below our feet, don't you know?

An ant that will be pierced by a woman's impartial needle. A magnificent woman. They say she got married by making phrases from the gospel vibrate: all the men heard seductive declarations in those mild words, those sentences that concealed the world's eroticism.

The men who are strongest join the army, the men who are strongest rape the women who are left behind, the wives of their fleeing enemies.

A soldier with a very red face forcefully lowers his manly pants to the ground. Forcefully his hands remove the dress, as if yanking back curtains to reveal an anatomical oddity: large breasts, quivering. The man's face is even redder now, and his penis is red as well. Red matter fornicates with a weak woman for a long time. It's Friday, and there's still a tree out in the yard, even though tanks are rolling through the streets. Johana isn't the woman beneath the soldier, but she heard about what happened to the woman beneath the soldier.

The noise heard while reading a book was the noise of airplanes in the sky. They don't bomb during the day, said Klaus.

Klaus set aside the book and looked directly at the noise. This isn't the sound of reading, he said. Nor is it the natural sound of the sky.

The planes had infiltrated nature's heights and were frightening.

There aren't any sailors, the sailors are all gone. They closed the sea.

There's a boat anchored in the water. It never leaves its place.

When it comes to philosophy, quick solutions should be reduced to a minimum. Careful study comes to you in old age: this sort of slowness is disappearing everywhere. May unending slowness abound.

Children with blank notebooks are content. In childhood, attempts are what matter.

A fragment of a news report becomes the starting point for a poem. Johana is quiet and the newspaper in her hands is unquiet. Who was killed today?

In the morning tanks appear to be unique objects, things that were created for the sake of making the streets hygienic. They clean the plazas, clean up the trash in the plazas. They clean up language in the plazas and cafés, and they clean up language because when the tanks pass by, men speak softly. Have you noticed that? It's Johana who's saying this to Klaus.

You've never seen a tank at work. This country is still perfect, this street is still perfect; no bomb has ever blown up near you.

It's good to have our enemies this close, driving down our streets in tanks; this way we can be sure that we're not going to be bombed.

Tanks pass by in the streets. The streets are named for our heroes. They don't understand our language; they don't know how to pronounce the names. They stumble on the pronunciation, they can't put the accents on the right syllables. Tanks don't have time to learn languages.

Klaus left his job, but just today. He works in a typography shop, and what's more he's an editor; he wants to publish books that upset the tanks.

This isn't a book, it's a little bomb.

You want to upset tanks with prose?

A snail, though just barely, since it's so small, passed beside Klaus, right next to his feet.

Look at how snails just barely move, said Klaus. Johana laughed.

Klaus suddenly raised his foot and forcefully crushed the snail. The sound was audible.

Why did you do that?

Klaus didn't reply.

To see nothing is to remain hidden.

There's too much asphalt in this country. Courageous men no longer have enough forest to hide themselves in.

A third of the men of the city were in hiding. The tanks didn't like the men that were in hiding. But the victors still displayed a certain ambivalence. They passed by in the streets and sometimes they smiled, while at other times they were cruel.

Yesterday they threatened to smash Klaus's glasses. Klaus kneeled; he kissed a man's boots.

Klaus recalled his childhood: he felt ashamed whenever he didn't know how to solve an algebra problem. Red-faced, assigning numbers to the left of a symbol and other numbers to the right of the same symbol. Those who could solve equations were heroes to him at that age. The eras in which we admire mathematicians are good eras.

Klaus hadn't felt ashamed when he kissed the right boot of the soldier. Later, yes. Removed from the action. Because when you're afraid you aren't ashamed, or the shame occupies less space than the fear, which is enormous. And for that reason it doesn't exist.

Only later on did he remember how he used to feel ashamed, standing in front of the chalkboard with an equation on it, the teacher staring at him, and not knowing how to get out of the situation. He had the sensation of being in a labyrinth; each equation was a labyrinth from which he didn't know how to escape.

I don't know how to solve this, said little Klaus. And it was then that he saw the teacher start to smile.

The teacher didn't smile much. He never smiled. He only smiled when a student made an error or when a student lowered his arms and said: I don't know how to solve this.

The teacher would then give the order for Klaus to lower his pants, and would tell him to bend over the desk, bum in air. He hit Klaus with a thick piece of wood. Hit him three times, hard. And Klaus hated numbers three times as much.

Shame doesn't exist in nature. Animals know the law: strength, strength, strength. The weak ones fall and do what the strong ones want. A flood, a downpour, a mammal that's heavier and faster than a mammal that's smaller. Primates, reptiles, big fish and small fish, waterfalls: have you ever seen an animal fall? There isn't the least hint of compassion between animals and water; ever since the world began the sea has been swallowing up dogs by the thousands. There isn't the least hint of compassion between water and plants, between crumbling soil and tiny animals that have just been born. Nature goes along with what's strong and the city goes along with what's strong: What's to doubt? What do you want?

There aren't any unjust animals, don't be an idiot. There aren't unjust floods or evil landslides. Injustice isn't part of the elements of nature; a dog, yes, and a tree and a body of water, but not injustice. If injustice turned into an organism—a thing that can die—then, yes, it would be a part of nature.

Man wanted to introduce into nature things invented by the weak; the weak invented injustice, so that they could later invent compassion. But not even the calmest waters can fathom the meaning of injustice. Do you think it's possible to surpass the benevolence of a chemical substance that can be rendered as simply as H_2O? Don't be an idiot. Look at the tanks: shoot with them or against them. Life during wartime means only one of two things: with them or against them. If you don't want to die, kiss the boots of the strongest, that's all there is to it.

Meanwhile, the unclean heavenly bodies maintain their gentle harmony.

Johana looks out the window. Klaus, her lover, hasn't arrived yet. So long as her lover hasn't arrived, the woman doesn't leave the window. Windows exist because lovers exist, and because those lovers aren't home yet. Windows cease to exist when the people you love return home. Look at the cold, the storm outside.

Klaus still hasn't returned. Will Klaus come back with the two arms he left with?

The world sometimes amputates the arms of men who are on the exterior side of the window. Look at the world, the world's got a blade.

Chapter II

1

Klaus is a tall man. He met Johana because he peered over the top of a very green hedge, peered over a spring month that was even greener than the hedge. They used to joke:

If you weren't so tall, I wouldn't have seen you over the hedge.

And Klaus would say to Johana:

If I weren't so tall the hedge would have been shorter.

Klaus believed in destiny more than Johana did. However, a single effect can never be realized by two separate changes to the world occurring in the past. If Klaus had been shorter, this would constitute a change to the world. If the hedge were also shorter, there would then be two changes to the world. If two different facts came to exist in the past, then the same outcome couldn't have occurred. Destiny has its own logic. Complex calculations are necessary in order to perceive what could have happened in place of what actually happened. There are too many possibilities for the same thing to happen every time. The world is varied and long-lasting. The world should be a tunnel, which you enter in the morning and exit at night. Without ramifications. An organized system of pipes, like the ones in houses. You turn on the faucet and water comes out. Or it doesn't. There are only two possibilities.

Just a little water can come out or it can be a lot, said Klaus, however, there are always variations between no and yes.

You're not a woman, said Johana. You're unaware of certain concepts, and of certain dances.

Klaus was a tall man and he liked working in the city. He dressed as if unaware of the clothes he was wearing: Or had only recently become aware, joked Johana. Poorly fitting pants, hair that seemed made of some other substance; Hair that doesn't belong to the head it's on, said Klaus, plus he wore impossibly mismatched colors. Johana would say: I'm holding out hope that you'll become a painter, and she'd laugh. Klaus entered his clothes as if they were a messy hotel room. Before the war, the two of them had fun together.

Meanwhile, Klaus published perverse books.

When Klaus was on the exterior side of the window, he was a small man. Johana would squint her eyes, forcing them to see, anxious. Eyes are like microscopes, amplifying things; waiting with the fear that something has happened to someone else is often like this too.

As a child, Johana would sound out words aloud so that her mother could hear her. Johana's mother was a madwoman. She had hallucinations that disrupted the normalcy of their lives. Johana's mother had once slashed her own vagina with a knife. Ever since that day, her family had understood that it wouldn't be possible for her to spend an entire day alone. They were afraid of her.

Johana's mother got worse in the spring, no one knew why. At the house there was a small garden with a large tree and a hedge. Johana's mother liked to trim the hedge, a completely level hedge calmed her. But Johana's mother couldn't trim the hedge evenly. She had what Johana called unhappy vision. Vision that doesn't want to see well. Vision that deteriorated, but not for physiological reasons. How to explain it? She just didn't see well.

It was because of this hedge that Johana saw Klaus for the first time, he who, in that first instance, was a tall man whom the hedge couldn't conceal.

Johana's mother was named Catharina and she was still alive and still crazy.

Klaus now dealt with her as best he could. He tried to remember that it was because of Catharina trimming the hedge crookedly that Johana had decided, that day, to trim the hedge. And had peered over it.

Catharina, Johana's mother, screamed.

She loved machines, substances with predictable outcomes.

Catharina calmed down when they put her hands in hot water.

Catharina loved chairs. She would sit down in one chair, then another.

Sometimes Johana would catch Catharina with a needle, trying to stick it into a machine. A radio, for example.

The radio is on.

But Catharina liked machines, liked messing with them. She wanted to insert herself into that cold life, but there was a perverse element to this behavior: Catharina would put the tip of the needle in boiling water, then she'd take the needle over to the radio or some other machine and try to stick it in one or another of its orifices. The difference in temperature excited her.

2

Catharina was a widow. Johana was her only daughter and Klaus was Johana's first boyfriend. There weren't many people connected to that house, where a level hedge had allowed Klaus to enter into the beginnings of love with Johana.

Catharina would sometimes utter some crazy idea. Through the window, she saw the tanks passing by in the street, and said that she wanted to stick a needle, its tip burnt, into a tank. She said that the tanks had countless chinks in them. She wanted to mend the tanks. Make them shoot more slowly. Or make them shoot the opposite way, inwardly. With a needle I could make the war explode from the outside in instead of inside out, said Catharina.

3

Klaus returned that day. Johana welcomed him with anxiety and a kiss. Their love was incomplete because the war had begun in the midst of it. War interrupts. Klaus was a tall man without any particular fondness for the fatherland, he'd spit on it if he had to, but he was willing to die for his books and his habits.

Some of Klaus's friends had already been killed. Some of Klaus's friends had already killed or attempted to kill. Klaus himself had remained neutral. They haven't set foot in my typography shop yet, said Klaus.

Klaus was a tall man who had read books. Klaus detested action, and dirt disgusted him. He started to like gardens after he looked at Johana over the hedge. Klaus said that during wartime a man should become a deaf-mute to the extent it was possible. And remain calm.

Klaus was from a rich family, the Klumps. His father—Mikhael Klump—was the owner of two factories. Money, he said, shouldn't suffer influence from changing maps. The invasion doesn't exist if they haven't interfered with our money, was one of his sayings.

Klaus had distanced himself from his parents, deciding to publish books that contested the economic and political systems of the time, but when the war started Klaus drew close to his family again.

Johana loved Klaus and was happy for him to continue his normal life, even though the streets were full of tanks and some of his friends had been killed. But sometimes Johana had unpleasant thoughts about Klaus. Nevertheless, she loved him.

4

No one loves a coward, which merely means that while you're in love with someone, you're unable to see their cowardice.

One day Johana was returning from the grocery store with three very expensive apples when she heard, in the middle of a street that was blocked-off and almost devoid of people, an orchestra playing songs she didn't recognize. There were no words, but the music was not from her country. This music isn't from here, thought Johana, starting to run swiftly toward home, and while she ran she cried.

Music is a strong symbol of humiliation. If those who've just arrived impose their music on the ones already there, it's because the world has changed, and tomorrow you'll be a foreigner in the place that used to be your home. Once they start playing new music, it means they have occupied your home.

All peoples have the right to their music and to silence. They have the right to decide how they want to interrupt that silence. The right to choose which sounds they want, which words and which musical notes. But pay attention: there are no communal silences. That's very frightening.

Certain men said to their sisters: You should protect your pronunciation the way you protect your vagina.

Don't repeat a single one of their words.

Men protected their sisters, but Johana didn't have a brother. She had Klaus.

One day soldiers entered Johana's home and saw that Johana was beautiful and further saw that Johana had a crazy mother who didn't even understand those who spoke her own language, much less those who spoke a different language.

One soldier named Ivor looked at Johana the most; he looked at her more than the other soldiers who weren't named Ivor.

Ivor said, in the language that Johana was forced to understand: I'm coming back. Don't forget me.

Johana heard him. Catharina also heard him.

Two days later, Ivor and three soldiers forced their way into Johana's house; the soldiers held her down, and Ivor raped her.

Catharina was locked in the bedroom and heard sounds that she didn't understand; she passed the time by scratching lines in the door with a needle, then putting the needle into the lock as if it were a key.

When Klaus arrived hours later, he held Johana tight, and it was Klaus who opened the door to the bedroom where Catharina was. Catharina had fallen asleep and it was Klaus who put away the needle that lay on the ground next to Johana's mother's tranquil body. Klaus carefully grabbed the needle with two fingers.

A MAN: KLAUS KLUMP

PART II

Chapter III

1

Klaus opened the drawer that contained a silver silverware tray. He had weak gums from eating poorly. Personality is a masterpiece that's constructed day and night. It takes longer than a few months, more time than it takes to build a palace. Personality is a task you enter into, it requires real effort.

Klaus's gums were very red. There was blood on Klaus's lower gum. Vitamins are important for the sentences you speak. Klaus now spoke with faulty grammar, he spoke confusedly. He lacked vitamins in his gums and his sentences had lost their former precision. He no longer discoursed promptly and aptly. His sentences were approximations, attempts. Language deprived of vitamins is incompatible with reality. Klaus opened the drawer that contained a silver silverware tray. He grabbed the silver silverware tray. He put it into a sack. Klaus said that the landscape had become unclean. There were no more reputable passions, with the exception of the desire for vengeance.

At some point, butterflies become repugnant. Beauty in a minuscule airplane, and too colorful. Klaus liked to snatch butterflies with his right hand and squeeze hard until a colorful substance dripped between his fingers. It's the only animal that retains its aesthetics even when crushed.

Klaus tested the light snow on the ground: it wasn't fake. Nature still resisted out there on the street, but in every direction people were telling lies. No one touches a dead horse when it's been out in the street for more than a week. Flies touch the dead horse, but neither men nor women nor children touch it. It's in the middle of the street, no cars are driving past anymore, there are no charming couples strolling by under parasols. There's a wall between last year and today. An incredibly high wall: no one understands what happened. How do you build a wall in time? How do you fence off, inside people's heads, the things that have occurred?

Klaus moved from place to place each night.

A military orchestra ascends the city's most important building and their music descends like airplanes poised to attack. They transform music into a plague, into a form of sickness that travels through air.

Women and children become afraid of music. This music announces the orchestra. They arrive at the top of the street and the women and children sink into their chairs. And the sea no longer exists.

It's obvious that this is impossible: not even a hundred thousand military machines could forcefully disturb the sea. But there are those who believe that the military orchestra goes out to sea in boats, and that they play out on the water. Water contaminated by music. The fish get sick. There's plague in a teacup just because of the music they're playing at the far end of the road. And mothers no longer get upset when soldiers rape their daughters. The old women kiss the soldiers, they don't cry after they leave; they make dinner, they tell their daughters: Just keep going, it's essential that we get this meal ready; Make the bed, they say. And their sons will be proud that the women didn't cry.

Chapter IV

1

Klaus is a tall man. He was a man that women liked to see over the tops of level hedges.

A storm. You don't even have two coins with which you can pretend to buy it. Nature is a woman, only she endures for longer and is more resistant. Look at the grass in the yard that's grown taller than some dogs. The hedge is crooked, but this time it wasn't Catharina: it was something unpredictable that never ceases.

Klaus was playing chess with another man, Alof. Alof had a bucketful of flutes and that bucket was all that remained of his History: Alof, before the tanks, had owned a music shop. They'd burned his house down, his wife had been taken. Alof, facing Klaus, was playing chess, and to his right was the bucket containing more than fifteen flutes, which he'd saved from his former home.

They no longer know music, these flutes.

Alof had never played again. There was too much music. The military orchestra ceaselessly circulated throughout the city. They had musicians who swapped places throughout the day, and the music played ceaselessly from seven in the morning until ten at night. Either we learn new rhythms to accompany the dawning of a new day, or we refuse to learn them.

In the forest the birds sympathized with the men who were playing chess. The birds sympathized, mutely, with the bucketful of flutes. Black bucket full of pale flutes.

Don't lose the bucket, Alof.

I won't lose the bucket, because my wife is in there too.

Alof was burly, he was a muscular man. Oh, how he once played instruments with those muscles and that strength! Alof used to say:

When I play music I make an effort to tone down my strength.

Alof was able to carry a thick tree trunk all by himself. Alof carried Klaus in his arms with extraordinary ease. Alof quickly snatched a lizard that was crawling near his feet and in one motion tore the lizard in half.

The bucket of flutes next to Alof.

In the forest there were no good times and Alof never played the flute during bad times. They asked him to play something, but Alof took the bucket everywhere he went and never played.

One night Klaus gave Alof a kiss on the forehead, and Alof immediately began to cry and for a minute Klaus didn't let go of him. Like you do with children.

Alof played chess with Klaus for hours on end. They were two players.

There were no trees in the forest. Nor hedges. Klaus sometimes laughed to himself for having previously thought that there would be some more or less level hedges in the forest.

The forest isn't so orderly, it never was.

Klaus said that they should build a hedge around the whole forest so that he could be seen above it by pretty women. Alof on the other hand expressed himself much more coarsely. How is it that someone like that can be a musician?

You must be indifferent to words in order to pay close attention to sounds.

Destiny isn't an apparition, it's a thing that advances. Time never lets anything fall out of itself. It isn't a sack.

An attack on a building shakes it; the men are preparing a bomb. Alof doesn't know a thing about explosions, he was a musician. First he played the trumpet, then the flute. You aren't going to lose that bucket, are you?

Put some water in the bucket and drown those instruments, they're useless out here. Sometimes there are small fires in the forest, and your bucket only serves to remind you of things. And it's no longer useful for you to remember anything, memory is very different when you have to keep your mind on combat.

Alof wasn't a warrior, he didn't know how to make a bomb; Klaus didn't either, but he was more practical.

After all this, said Klaus, we'll play chess, and I'll let you win.

Alof had never won a game against Klaus. They were evenly matched games, and they almost always tied; sometimes Klaus won. But Alof never did.

You have less anger than I do, you can still manage to think calmly, said Alof to Klaus.

Chapter V

1

A siren blares. A military siren isn't a peaceful instrument that makes women dance. This siren makes women cry.

A mother lost her baggage in a station. The baggage was her six-year-old daughter.

You lost your baggage, lady.

The mother is crying because she doesn't know where her six-year-old daughter is: They took her from me!

They control all baggage. What was your daughter wearing?

These days, when you see bones on a plate, it makes a great impression. There was a chicken to be split between seven men. Alof wasn't hungry.

Two days earlier they'd dug up some bodies and there were things that had stayed in his head and wouldn't leave.

I can't eat this.

Klaus said that at least there are no floods in the forest. There are only two places in the world: places that can catch fire and places that can flood. We're in the former.

The various pigments of fire ended up painting the pathways black. Klaus picks up a book that has a silver fork for a bookmark.

What did you do with the rest of the silverware?

Klaus doesn't reply. In the forest, both joy and answers are always slow to come. No one drops anything: the landscape at half the height of men slides between the high branches and the ground. The objects that the men are carrying stay at that half-height: between their heads and the grass. A cup to drink from. A small plate. And Klaus still has a ring on his finger.

Nature never takes a side, and this disgusts me.

Alof didn't want it to rain today because the rain would make it harder to go down to the city and steal, but it's raining today nonetheless.

If we defeat the tanks, let's turn them against nature and fire away.

You wouldn't hit it, said Klaus, laughing.

No one saw a big bat fly past, but there are black animals that cause things to happen at night.

I never notice the animals. Alof is drinking under the black sky: This is the sky's true color, today I don't doubt it.

Alof vomited with his body seated and his throat bent over the grass, black with night.

This reminds me of my barber. He said that I have stupid hair, that it doesn't grow enough; it doesn't turn him a profit.

Alof had just vomited, a disgusting smell wafting from his mouth, and Klaus laughed:

At a moment like this you think of your barber.

Alof suddenly took a flute from the black bucket.

You're not going to play like this, your mouth is disgusting.

I am going to play like this, said Alof. He held the flute for the first time in months and, his stomach turning from the taste of his mouth, he began to play.

When he finished, he turned and said: Mozart.

You need to wash your mouth, said Klaus. I'll go get some water.

Chapter VI

1

Johana isn't alone in the bedroom, Catharina fell asleep beside her on the bed not too long ago, and Johana is masturbating.

The two of them live alone. The yard now belongs to the street. The hedge is flawless now, it does what the days wish of it. Certain animals become comic in the middle of the confusion that abandonment has wrought. The dead horse is still dying out in the street. Thousands of flies search for material things in the horse's back. Thousands of flies, there are thousands of flies ganging up together. No one strolls through the street where an animal that once was so strong and proud has flies defecating in its eyes. No one is curious to see how a thing that was once a horse is transformed into something that is strangely still warm, yet repulsive. The afternoon continues on, certain impressive colors are still beautiful back beyond the horse, and the eyes like them. The sunset.

A train derailed, say the newspaper headlines, and the food that was on its way here was stolen by the guerrillas. At school there's no one so barbaric as to pay attention to books: the teachers hold the children close and give them advice about how to make the quickest escape whenever the dangerous sounds commence. A child is hungry, and the teacher slaps him. The teacher cries. The child asks her for a story. The teacher tells him a story and the child falls asleep on her lap. He's very hungry and still he sleeps.

Out on the landscape, machines have replaced animals. Machines don't leave feces on the sidewalks. Women used to be appalled by dog excrement on the sidewalk. They used to say that the owners lacked common courtesy. Today women are appalled when five soldiers enter their houses and grab them and rape them, one soldier after another.

Machines aren't chubby. It's an unsuitable combination of words. An illiterate man sits behind a machine that can kill a hundred people at once. The tanks are parked and arranged throughout traffic circles and beside a fountain. An enormous tank is a masterpiece next to water. How simple water is, how insignificant, next to powerful technology.

A tank is an extraordinary stone. A perfected stone. Even the children of certain women who are raped by soldiers, even those children like to approach, on Sundays, those unequivocal, mechanical stones, those tall machines.

In the house there was a coffee machine that made unnecessary noises and then that machine disappeared; the child looks up at the tank, and believes that this machine came to take the place of the coffee machine that was stolen from his home. It was stolen along with the child's father. This machine will bring back the coffee and my father.

Children are treated well. Just like the infrastructure of the buildings in the city center. That which is useful is treated well. And that which isn't dangerous is useful. But there are different types of children: for example those whose bodies are already erotic, and violent as well. They play stupid and steal important things from the big machines.

There are more than fifteen children out there with Alof and Klaus. But many of them are dead. They were buried as the heads of living men looked down upon them, and with other children, curious, riding piggyback on these men's shoulders so they could see the graves.

Klaus recalled that as a child he melted ants by holding a lit match close to them. The ants melted quickly, curling up into themselves and then disappearing. Klaus remembered this today because he saw a photograph in the newspaper of the aftermath of a bombing. News sometimes arrived weeks late, but all the sentences remained in the present.

The rotting horse in the middle of the street, covered with thousands of flies, hadn't appeared in the newspaper even once. That street wasn't of any interest: it was straight, the tanks could hardly be pleased by a street now centrally occupied by the remains of a rotting horse. The horse's head is empty, it's smaller than the head of a bird. The horse's head is a black bucket, empty inside.

2

Johana looked after Catharina's hygiene. She'd wash Catharina first with what little water she had. She washed her mother's entire body; she carefully washed her mother's vagina, which still had a wound that wouldn't scar over. Her fingers carefully in Catharina's vagina, with an obsessive, careful attention to hygiene. Johana then bathed herself in the same water. She was always second. The first bath was for Catharina, her mother, who was crazy.

I'll wash myself in the second bath, said Johana to her mother.

There was no water, there was very little water. But there was fire, fire was easy. There were matches, the tanks were parked now, but there were some very hot things, new animals in the city, a metallic organism, tall, too, almost as tall as a giraffe, how many meters tall? There were birds that flew below the uppermost part of the tank. It was a standard by which to measure the city. Below the tanks, above the tanks. Certain distant mountains were hopeful things, because they greatly surpassed the height of the tanks.

If you punctured a hot machine through one side to the other, and if you were able to peek through it, as if through a lock in a door, the world would be more livable. To see the landscape through the tank.

The men were cutting through the underbrush. A cultured man was talking about painters. Klaus was urinating and was happy to see the strong, yellow urine come out. A man can urinate standing up and pretend that he's urinating on top of the tanks.

Alof laughed.

There were stupid, black animals even in the daytime. Not all animals are only black at night, or just in the firelight. Fire throws off the balance between night and the certain light of day. It brings night to things, brings it inside of them.

We are in a place where men are afraid of fire. The soldiers intentionally burn the forest, but the soldiers don't want to mistreat the animals, they want to catch Klaus, Alof, and the other men. There are still four children who are alive, and now they're combatants. They're ready.

An insignificant man becomes powerful when he's angry. And there wasn't a single weak man among Klaus's companions.

Alof's breath had a sickly smell. Alof's gums were extremely swollen and red. Alof said that he felt well and was still strong when it came to wood; he carried a thick tree trunk and laughed at his own red gums.

Klaus met Herthe during one of his secret trips down to the city. On that night, this woman slept with Klaus. Herthe, Herthe.

I'm poisonous, said Klaus, hide me, and don't talk about me.

On that morning Klaus was captured. A number of soldiers entered the house that belonged to the woman named Herthe, too many for it to mean mere desire for a woman. Klaus put his hands up. He was naked. Herthe didn't say a word. The soldiers turned their backs on her and took Klaus.

Chapter VII

1

In prison, Klaus's penis is the source of derision. Another prisoner slobbers on the nape of Klaus's neck and repeatedly sings vulgar songs. Civilization ended there: the prisoners were ancient, living but half-crazy; some had committed domestic crimes. There was no remorse. Klaus was in a cell with seven men and none of them noticed his health, the righteousness of his hatred. They knew nothing of the recent tanks, or the intruding horse that had been rotting for months in the middle of a street: the prisoners were old, crazy people who never opened their eyes.

The man with slobber on his chin is singing a schoolyard song, repeating it fifteen times. Klaus is alone. His penis is a source of derision. They are all naked: seven naked men with him in the same cell and one of them coming over to slobber on the nape of his neck. They were crazy. Another one wouldn't stop whistling, his back turned to the rest of the group.

And now one of them has a razor. Klaus tries to stay away, go off to another corner, but one of them has a razor and it's the one who slobbered on the nape of Klaus's neck.

Your dick hasn't been tried out yet, said the man. Klaus didn't know what this meant.

Frightened and backed up against a wall, he tried to give off a respectful air. He didn't dare look at the other men's penises, but ever since he'd arrived his had been a source of derision. He didn't understand what was happening; he took quick glances but couldn't spot any difference. He was imprisoned, and he passed the time trying to compare his penis with those of the other seven men. They were crazy.

The man with the razor came closer; three others approached as well. Klaus quickly turned around and the man with the razor slobbered on the nape of his neck with his lips. Klaus tried to react, but the men grabbed hold of him; the other man still had his mouth on the nape of Klaus's neck—he heard someone whistling still—and still had the razor, while many men held him tight, and he tried to get away. Someone forcefully grabbed his penis, pulled down on it, and it was then that he again felt, with disgust, the slobber on the nape of his neck that would not stop.

2

Men who don't experience normal joy are dangerous men. Look at the way they laugh, the things they laugh at.

The cold is deadly in certain ill-equipped bones. Few clothes. There's a smell of semen, urine, and excrement. Vomit is rare. On certain nights there's sleep.

Even a small stone would cheer up the room. The architecture isn't complex; the area is flat, with no surprises, and there are times when a man would give all his money to build a small ledge or hole in the cell, some variation within that place.

There is neither fog nor rain. Nature is something that's described in stories. Some men, when they're not laughing, tell stories.

In the morning there is a polite, firm tension. The fleeting light calms the madmen: a lot of light, no; total darkness, also no. The best part of the day is when the day begins.

Klaus is able to think more clearly than the others, but he has already realized that it's only because he came much later than they did. One of the madmen used to be a writer. Six months ago Klaus was a publisher.

Klaus understands what's going on here, or nearly understands. These men have been imprisoned for many years. While he was a publisher. While he savored exotic sweets, hot from the kitchen. While he complained about a bulky, uncomfortable chair that his parents insisted on keeping.

It almost justifies the tanks: the tanks came to get these men out of here. But the men are still here months after the tanks arrived. Is the horse still out there in the middle of the street?

Sunday is a day that carries friendship around on its shoulders. People used to get mixed up with one another because their suits were similar, and on the street which is now the street with the horse, merchants calmly smoked cigarettes. Whether they sold very little, or whether they sold a lot.

There are infiltrations of metal throughout the entire city. Before, there were those things you used to call "garden plots." In terms of color, gray is much more common to war than green. And you know this.

Money had no value for the madmen. Klaus had cash, but now he was naked; when you're naked you don't have any money. Money becomes extremely abstract when eight naked men inhabit the same space. And are trying not to die. But even so, it's still important. The men quickly found out that Klaus's parents were very rich. They were the Klump family. And the man who kept slobbering on the nape of Klaus's neck was now his friend.

Chapter VIII

1

There's a different sort of dust in the city. Clarity means that you can be seen, and that's not good. Clarity has become a bad thing. Clarity is something that smacks you like a cudgel, not something that settles upon you.

The feminine things in the city become aggressive. The legs of young women are no longer meaningful. There are no professions, but skills have increased. Men have become primitive, each one a general with his own strategy. The days aren't daily. The days are divided into months; morning and night are two different worlds, and you travel between them only through violence.

Herthe was the woman who had kissed Klaus. The soldiers had arrived and interrupted the lovers.

Herthe was a hard woman. She never thought about what had happened. She had an understanding with the soldiers. Her buttocks had already sweetly delivered many guerrillas into their hands. Herthe was a woman who wanted to keep up her garden plot.

Before the tanks entered the city and the horse rotted in the middle of the road for months, before that, said Herthe, before that, I had a garden plot. Like many of the city's inhabitants. And Herthe still had her garden plot.

And not just her garden plot: Herthe had living, fully intact parents by her side. And Herthe still had a twelve-year-old brother, living, healthy, intact, well-treated and well-received by the soldiers.

Herthe was a pretty woman. Herthe had a bedroom all to herself now. Before the arrival of the soldiers, Herthe had shared a bedroom with her twelve-year-old brother and Herthe's parents had slept in the other bedroom. But now it was the opposite, her brother slept in the same bedroom as her parents, because Herthe needed the other bedroom so she could receive men.

Few of the soldiers had slept with Herthe. Only the ones with the most power, and those were the ones who protected her.

And every man from the resistance who slept with Herthe only slept with her once, because he always woke up surrounded by soldiers. How many had she turned in to the soldiers? Who knows: seven, eight?

But one day Herthe arrived home and her parents told her that her brother had disappeared. He was twelve years old, and his family called him Clako. He had run off to the forest.

2

Alof, mighty Alof, had for years taught some of the city's children in one of the practice rooms in his music shop. Clako, Herthe's brother, had been his student.

Clako wasn't a good musician, he would never be a good musician. He was too restless. But Alof remembered him. He was a strong kid. He knew how to hate like an adult, and attack. Alof had always told Clako's family: He's not going to be a musician, but in a few years I'll merely be one of his followers.

But now Clako was at Alof's side, hiding out in the forest. And Herthe had just found out that her brother had disappeared, Alof thought.

There's no mystery to it: it's just that certain people don't like indecency. The heart isn't just a tender part of the innards. There's a moral system somewhere in that soft part of the body. And a system is something thick, something that remains firmly in place: a stone. A metal room.

These private, intimate courts of law garner more respect than a mountain. You can't look squarely at the things you're made of and that retain their bulk in the face of great change. You are the one who decides how many utensils you're going to put on top of reality. You choose the instrument, and you choose the sharpened point that saves and the sharpened point that kills.

There's no charity in wartime, and pain loses its value abruptly. In times of boredom, pain is a matter of diamonds, capable of shocking a multitude.

Not so during wartime. Pain is no marvel in wartime; animals suffer, get limbs amputated, and continue to advance, because complaints are for laggards.

In wartime, bodies are closer together, those of friends as well as those of enemies.

Fingernails are black. Words change very little, your vocabulary in extreme situations isn't made up of more than fifty elements.

Dance with your mouth open to obtain a different air in your movements. To dance is to gain confidence in your body. Dance well so you can kill nimbly.

The murderer knows the right steps to the dance. Agility is a notion that quickly passes from the white world to the black world. To dance well is to train for survival.

And no one wants to learn scientific things unless they're useful. Anything that doesn't explode is useless science during these times. Does knowledge of the laws of physics allow you track someone down better or faster?

Weapons are all that's left of a series of instruments and experiments. There are no chemical formulas for substances, you're only interested in chemical formulas for actions. The chemical formula for shooting with precision at great distances. You can hit the nape of the neck of another person with a bullet depending on the angle of your elbow.

Geometry exists only through dangerous angles, angles that point at a soldier's head. For example, there are no angles for harvesting fruit from a tree. We're at war.

Seven months after his arrest, Klaus received a visit from his parents. Klaus's parents were still living in the same house as always. They'd been businesspeople before the soldiers invaded, and after the invasion they got into other sorts of business. They were respected, and they respected others. No one had touched anything of theirs. Brutality is luxurious and fine in the eyes of rich people; it's nothing new.

Klaus was dressed in order to receive his parents. But he still had his body. And his body was skinny and his eyes were different, un-equivocal: they knew what had to be done. Klaus the prisoner was a man who no longer hesitated.

His parents were dressed in their normal style. Klaus remembered the coat that his father was wearing. Klaus had helped him pick it out. How long had it been? Two years, a year?

Klaus's mother was dressed in a bold color. Klaus's mother didn't say anything. Klaus saw the jewel that always hung from her neck.

Klaus's father said:

We'll get you out of here whenever you want. We have the money. Everything has been set up. You'll come work for us. Business is going well. If you come work for us you'll soon forget all of this. Life has returned to normal. They're building something in the city center. Not a single member of the resistance remains. Things have changed since you've been in here. There almost aren't any soldiers anymore. Everything is returning to normal. People are working like they did before. Business is getting better and better. Transportation, too. Goods come in and out quickly. There's talk of a new railway that would expand the city. Families in cars can once again be seen cruising the streets.

Klaus's father stopped talking.

Klaus's eyes were lowered and he remained motionless for a few seconds. Then he said:

Let me think. Come back next week. But come alone, he requested, without mother.

Klaus's father smiled. He stood up. Klaus's mother followed him.

I'll be back next week to pick you up, said his father.

A week later, Klaus's father entered the prison alone. He came dressed in a light-colored suit and a light-colored tie. He walked with vigorous steps, he was happy. He sat down in the visitors' room to wait for his son.

He saw Klaus approaching from way in the back. Wearing inmate's clothes, drawing closer. Klaus's father instinctively looked at Klaus's right hand: it was bleeding. He couldn't understand what was happening. He kept looking at Klaus's hand. In his right hand, Klaus had a shard of glass, which he was gripping tightly. Klaus drew closer. He was now five meters from his father. His father was about to ask him what had happened to his hand; Klaus raced the last few steps, raised his right hand, and forcefully drove the glass into his father's eye. With all the force he could muster.

Chapter IX

1

It's the day of Herthe's wedding to one of the most powerful officers in the army.

Herthe is happy. The officer is a handsome, intelligent man.

Brutality has assumed its place and no longer offends anyone.

A dream is an unfinished day, said Ortho, the groom, to his friend. Actions are interrupted, and all that was accomplished disappears, there are no effects like there are out here, in the true day.

Ortho was a sensible man. A reader of philosophy, and a man who disemboweled animals with his own hand, with just the blade of a pocketknife a few centimeters long. He knew that there was a time to interpret and a time to slice open the neck of an animal with a single slash.

A war hero, he quoted philosophical texts and lines of poetry.

He'd been wounded many times by members of the resistance. When a wound doesn't touch your memory, it is insignificant, he used to say. The men remembered hearing him, in the infirmary, recite entire poems that he had known since childhood. He withstood pain by exercising his memory. It was his method. Never stop thinking—if, in addition to blood, we let memory flow out of our bodies, we die.

At the wedding, a bottle in Ortho's hand, raised as if it were the crown of a king.

He started pouring wine onto the heads of his friends. The other men accepted it, laughed.

A woman with ample breasts, seated at one of the wedding tables, is laughing endlessly. The others recount anecdotes. The woman with the massive breasts pisses herself from laughing so much;

the others see it and laugh even more. The woman can't stop laughing and the urine is visible on her skirt all down to her feet.

The younger boys devour more sweets than fruit. A boy smells a young girl's perfume and his penis becomes aroused.

Two adolescents are stealing silverware and for that reason they want to leave as quickly as possible, but their parents are having fun and hope to continue.

On the balcony facing the garden, six meters above the ground, a band is preparing for the dance to begin. Sounds of various instruments being tuned can be heard.

There's a coffee machine that's very popular. Some of the soldiers are drinking coffee at a ratio of one-tenth of the wine they drink. It's a way of controlling themselves. Coffee reduces the unhappiness that wine brings on, but it also reduces what happiness it brings too.

The number of women at the party is much greater than the number of men, despite all the soldiers. Nevertheless, from the beginning the women make less noise.

At the beginning of the banquet, macho stories are told: only with time and wine do feminine subjects earn some consideration. Because, after a certain point, wine softens the soldiers more than it excites them.

The band starts playing. Feminine shoulders stir in the vicinity of the soldiers.

Ortho says: Some of these men will only today realize that certain viscera, like the heart, are not imaginary and not just the invention of doctors.

In war, organs become fragile things, and skin and uniforms must hide them. Skin, uniforms, strategy, weapons, your army: all elements that conceal the viscera.

Ortho says: Some of these soldiers used flowers the same way that they used tall grasses and small mounds of earth: to hide themselves, to camouflage themselves. Today I see them look to flowers as a means of seduction.

Ortho says: Before, they were only interested in the opaque parts of things out in nature, but today they're also interested in the color of each thing. And they like the thing that they never liked before: transparency.

When you're happy, the skills required of you change, said Ortho.

For the last fifteen minutes, Ortho has been solving mathematical puzzles with his friend. They use the paper tablecloth to write down numbers and solve equations. Herthe lightly touches the back of her groom's neck. You drank too much, she says, laughing. You're solving mathematical equations at your own wedding.

Ortho almost doesn't hear her. He smiles, continues to bury himself in the numbers.

The music starts.

The women like clean dances, but the men don't mix hygiene with music. They've cleared away the indiscrete glasses of wine, but the lips of some of them are a drunk, reddish commotion. They have a strong smell. But the women greatly outnumber the men, and for that reason the women don't choose, they're chosen.

The women try to show off their clean gums, but some young women haven't been eating well. Food is something that's kept safe in cupboards. No one knows what's going to happen. A happy day is one of war's masterpieces. The war allows for unbelievable days. And today is one of those days.

Herthe is a happy woman. She loves her groom. Her groom is intelligent, armed public currency. She notices everything, she always noticed everything, no one needs to tell her which way each cog turns. She's happy because she's in love with a man who is intelligent public currency and is well-protected by the entire army. Herthe is no longer a little girl; her father has died, leaving behind her elderly mother, who has an illness that has turned her skin an embarrassing color. No one ever committed a single malicious act against her parents, and she knows that this is her victory. But her brother Clako hasn't been seen in four years, and Herthe knows that this is her mother's illness, and that this is her own defeat. However, today Herthe has new joys. Even her elderly mother is tapping her foot, hidden beneath the table, to the sound of the music.

A dance is an amorous machine. A dance is a machine that makes weddings half a year in advance. And the young women know this better than the men. And for that reason they don't stop, they don't want to sit down, they challenge any soldier who wants to rest. It's a second combat, and the women are much more ferocious. Like animals, they seduce the idiotic soldiers who complain about being tired.

Ortho, the principal man, isn't dancing. He's solving mathematical puzzles with his friend Jash, writing numbers and drawing geometric shapes on the paper tablecloth. Herthe sometimes passes by and kisses him on the head: You look like a scientist, she says.

The dance is a structure that grows larger. The music slowly undresses the young women, who, nevertheless, remain fully clothed.

Herthe dances with an officer. Ortho remains at Jash's side. Two other men have joined them. Now, the four of them gather around mathematical problems. They drink more wine.

Herthe dances with a young officer who starts getting aroused. Herthe notices. At the end of the song she stops, thanks him for the dance, and walks away. The young soldier grabs another woman; there are a lot of them, they're just waiting around. The young man's name is Ivor.

Herthe is heading over to the restrooms. She passes a number of young women who are excitedly hurrying back to the dance floor.

But the music stopped a few minutes earlier. It's an intermission. The musicians need to drink.

As she leaves the restroom, Herthe suddenly crosses paths with one of the musicians. She recognizes him immediately: it's her brother, Clako. He's a man now. How is it possible?

Clako says: I'm here to kill your husband. He's the most important officer remaining in the city. I hope you'll help me.

Clako stares attentively at Herthe.

Herthe, standing in front of her brother, says:

You need to go see Mother. She needs to see you. She's sick.

Clako doesn't hear her. I hope you'll help me, he says. I want you to take your husband out behind the restrooms at the end of the dance. I'll be there.

Then he turns his back on Herthe and walks off toward the other musicians.

2

The dance is still going on, but Ortho still hasn't danced.

A soldier is riding on the back of a pig and exposing himself. Ortho shoots him a quick smile that makes it clear he doesn't approve. The soldier calms down and walks away.

Ortho is talking about the war.

Trees turn browner. Animals become timid, and men get lost in it.

Women's skirts go up faster in wartime.

Herthe goes over to her mother, who is still motionless, seated, weak, watching. Herthe whispers into her ear: My little brother is alive. I'll tell you about it later.

Her mother gets flustered; Herthe smiles, shushes her warmly, and walks away.

Herthe is walking toward the dance again and puts her arms around Ortho, who's still at the table. She kisses his hair. She walks around a bit. Then she heads over to the dance.

The same young officer as before, named Ivor, casts a young woman aside hurriedly and once again walks toward Herthe. Herthe accepts his invitation.

The two of them dance again. The other young women have taken note of it, and some of the soldiers, too: Herthe is dancing too much with the officer named Ivor. And the handsome officer has had a lot to drink and is aroused.

Someone says to Ortho and the other officers who are seated: The brain does not make progress in combat. Reason is a useless, dangerous thing in combat.

It's that time when the men start to tell stories.

Ortho: Corpses were put in high places so that the enemies could see them clearly. Even our corpses. No one can tell if they're theirs or ours from a distance. Corpses on display are more frightening than tanks.

We captured an old lady who said she was the reincarnated spirit of a six-year-old girl. We all laughed.

The men are drinking wine. They're telling stories.

The body is transformed into an object, into a new substance. I've never been able to be near a dead body for more than a few minutes.

My mother had seven children. Five died. The other one is a teacher. He has an illness. He could never be a soldier. If I had an illness I wouldn't be a soldier either. We did everything together, my brother and I. We shared books with each other. Up until we were sixteen we read the exact same books, but ever since he was a child he had a cough.

We only parted ways because of the war. I joined the army and he stayed home, ill. Since the start of the war we began to read different books. I have no idea what kinds of books he reads now.

Ortho stopped talking. He had a little something to drink.

Your wife is calling for you, said one of the officers.

It's best not to leave such a beautiful woman alone for very long, said another.

Ortho stood up. He said: I'll leave a problem for you all to solve—and he began to draw on a blank space that remained on the paper tablecloth.

Who can connect four points with a single line? And he laughed.

Then he turned away from the table and headed toward his wife.

The couple dances together for the first time. Herthe looks radiant. Up in the balcony, the band keeps time steadily. They're intentionally playing a romantic song for the newlyweds, who hold each other tight. Herthe kisses Ortho once, then again. There's applause, little shrieks of encouragement. The band plays on.

The sun is beginning to disappear. The band stopped playing some time ago. No one knows yet if this is another intermission or the end of the music. Herthe is holding hands with Ortho; she leads him through the throng of guests. She leads him toward the back of the restrooms. They stroll around the building.

Herthe hastily kisses Ortho, who becomes aroused. Suddenly: a noise, and Herthe sees the face of her brother, Clako, who at that moment had just thrust a knife into Ortho's neck, and then he does it again, and once more, five, six times, mightily. Ortho is dead. He falls to the ground.

Almost silently.

Ortho is on the ground. Clako smiles at Herthe, makes the sign for silence with his finger and lips, goes to say something and then seems to hesitate, but suddenly Herthe starts screaming. And her screams summon the soldiers.

Clako remains motionless for a moment, he doesn't react. Then he turns around and starts to run, to flee.

It takes a few seconds for the soldiers to arrive on the scene. They see Ortho on the ground and quickly realize what has occurred. They run after the fleeing man. They shoot, then shoot again. They hit the fleeing man. Clako falls. The soldiers shoot again. Herthe orders them to stop: He's my brother! she screams.

Chapter X

1

Clako wasn't killed by the soldiers, but the bullets hit him in some vital places. Clako can't move his spine, he's unable to speak. He can only make a few unintelligible sounds. He can just move some of his fingers, and only with great difficulty. He's in a wheelchair. And Herthe, his sister, is the one who pushes him around.

Their elderly mother was happy to have her son back. She didn't understand what had happened and didn't want to understand. And despite the fact that she now had a disabled son who was completely dependent on others, even dependent on them to feed him, their elderly mother was happy. She knew she only had one or two more years to live. And her two children were in her house, taken care of. She knew Herthe well, she was her oldest child. She would never abandon her brother.

Herthe was the one who fed Clako. She patiently took the food from his plate and raised it up to his mouth. Their elderly mother was no longer capable of doing this.

The first few times, Clako refused to eat, spit the food out at Herthe, and shot her violent looks. He was nearly shaking from the tension that he created within himself. But at the end of the second day Clako started to accept the food that his sister gave him. There was no other way. He needed to eat. And there was no one else who could feed him. No one else who would make such a sacrifice, who would have such patience. And Clako needed to eat, he wanted to live.

No malevolent looks crossed Herthe's face, she treated him with care; she had a disabled brother, it was her duty to take care of him.

Their elderly mother would sometimes cry, she would get emotional. It's clear that she felt the two siblings were hiding some secret. She felt that the looks they gave each other weren't the same ones they used to give during their childhood spats, but the way that the sister helped her brother in everything made her emotional.

Clako was unable to communicate in any way. He only made grotesque sounds. His hands weren't even strong enough to write a single letter, and he no longer understood the words in a book or a newspaper. Clako was isolated, he could only feel things, that was all. It was as if he now only had two states of being: irritated or content.

Herthe, meanwhile, was considered a widow in the eyes of society. Her husband had been murdered at his own wedding. She was the widow of Ortho, one of the most respected and important officers in the army. She was treated very well by the people of the city.

However, Herthe was only twenty-eight years old. And she was still pretty.

Chapter XI

1

Klaus had black lips, as if he spoke a different language. He had lost his country and with this loss all of the old words had become obscene. They were black words. They burned your lips.

When Klaus was young he had been known for his prominent lips, indecent lips, as some of the young women used to say.

Klaus was in prison with Xalak, the man who salivated excessively, the man who had slobbered all over the nape of his neck, the man who was ruler of the cell. They had become friends. Xalak was the oldest, the leader. The two of them have been in the same cell for seven years. They talked to each other.

Words emerged like a black flood. Klaus was still a tall man, but he didn't speak the same way he used to. He had been a publisher of perverse books, but that was back in the days when water was still neutral.

Xalak said: Water was never neutral.

When Klaus was twenty years old he used to use binoculars to spy on women.

My lips are darkening at the same rate as the inside of my body, said Klaus, almost with a laugh. In fact, he had no idea what had happened to his lips. The other men told him: Your lips are black, and he had no reason to doubt them. One time he asked a guard to bring him a mirror, and he verified it: his lips were black.

A black flood. I should speak as little as possible.

Xalak was half-crazy and half-dead, as Klaus put it.

Xalak was very skinny, and tall, too. He had murdered a powerful man and his wife. That was more than fifteen years earlier.

They never would've done what they've done to me if I'd killed some unimportant man. And if I'd murdered someone like me, then I'd be laughed at.

Was Xalak there just to rob the house, or to kill? Nobody knows how to answer such questions when even the murderer himself hasn't answered. This was the case here.

Xalak would merely repeat over and over: I did what was necessary.

Xalak didn't talk about it, but the fear that he inspired in others was due, in part, to the striking manner in which he had killed the couple.

The house had been protected by two guards. You might be able to get in, but it would be difficult to get back out. Xalak had managed to get in.

Xalak was respected in prison because he'd killed a powerful man. But Klaus was also well known and feared. The story of his father's visit and his attack with the glass had made the rounds.

Xalak's fingers always smelled like wine, even though he hadn't had a drink in a long time. Xalak's fingers were red, slick, and long.

Xalak wasn't interested in news about the resistance or the war. He'd been in prison for many years. Many years before it all started.

Xalak would say that when he got out, he was going to kill another important man. He'd laugh: I've developed a habit of not being on the right side of things.

2

You don't dare spit on a wolf, but if necessary you'll piss right on the head of a dog. That's the difference.

Teeth are restless. Teeth bite into food; that's all that's left. With your teeth biting into meat so you don't die, your saliva envelops the food, and that's how I can speak. If I stop speaking I'll die. Hungry.

I sleep poorly. In prison they got rid of the sky. If they told me that the planets and stars had ceased to exist, I'd believe them. Even the rain. Sometimes I hear a sound that could be rain, but it could also be boots scraped against the ground, to clean off the mud.

From a distance, a soldier's boots scraping against the ground to clean off the mud can remind you of the sound of rain. Being far away from things is nauseating.

For me, History has ended. If they lock me up in a room for years, where is the country? No country ever came here to save me, I spit on the country; the country isn't a wolf that will bite you, it's a stupid, subservient landscape that just sits and takes it. You can piss on the country's head, like you can do to a well-trained dog, and it'll just take it: it'll wag its tail.

The wall is high, but if only on the other side there was the sea, and not just land and more land. The land uses pants and boots, and it disgusts me.

Tomorrow they say they're going to bring a prostitute with massive breasts in here, into the cell. They say that she's going to service us all, as many times as we want. Xalak says that he just wants her to watch them with each other. We've been here for years and we've never needed a woman, if a woman comes in here, she's going to be humiliated.

All the places where my people were must have different sounds now. Places change sounds depending on the people there. If there are more people speaking a different language at a certain place, that place changes: sounds are the things that change a place the most.

Even the women change their sounds depending on the men they have around them.

Johana must make different sounds, she must already speak a different language.

The passion behind your actions doesn't depend on money, but everything else depends on money. There are actions that are very poor but quite passionate, and at least the world resists in this way.

You may not have a single cent in your pocket, but you can still become extremely aroused.

If our enemies give our women flowers, that's a sign that we're in prison.

You should exercise your intelligence. Never let your head stop, even if your other appendages do. There are two organs that you should never allow to stop: the brain and the penis. That's what's said. They're the two main organs, and they're the two organs of arousal: they tell us how close we are to dying.

When you're in prison, one of the urges you get is to urinate on a tree. It's completely stupid, but I've thought about this countless times. With an engorged penis and a full bladder, to go up to a tree and urinate. That's it.

Here on the inside, nature wears boots and a uniform, and sometimes it's pleasant. And the hardest thing to take is when they're being pleasant. When our enemy is pleasant, it's a sign that we're completely inoffensive. You're so weak that even your enemy will help you out.

Xalak says that he's going to kill the woman with massive breasts that the guards promised to bring in to cheer up the men. The guards must have already had too much fun watching us with each other. They want some variety now. But they watch us, that's easy enough to see. They spy on us in here. Sometimes it even seems like we can hear them laugh.

The men awake. Today's the day that the woman with massive breasts is coming. She must be one of ours. They wouldn't even give us one of their prostitutes. At least we understand better the way the buttocks of our own women move. Of those who speak our language.

Women are from our own country when we understand the movements their buttocks make while they're getting screwed.

Here comes Xalak: he holds out his hand to me. I'm going to be your friend until I'm able to kill you, I think to myself.

Xalak held out his hand to Klaus and helped him to his feet. Klaus whispered in his ear: Today the two of us are going to escape. They just now told me. The fat prostitute is the one who's going to get us out of here. Prostitutes are the ones who save.

Chapter XII

1

Ivor, the officer with the attractive face, was a man who "frequented Johana," as they say. Ivor no longer took other soldiers with him, he didn't need to anymore. Johana was his lover now.

The soldiers respected "this." Johana accepted "this."

Ivor was the one who still managed to get medication for Catharina, Johana's crazy mother. Catharina was under control, but Johana was careful to make sure all the knives were out of reach, so she wouldn't cut herself. Catharina spent the entire day looking around for a needle. The two women hardly ever left the house.

Johana didn't know that Klaus had been imprisoned. Klaus had been missing ever since that one day. The day she was raped. They hadn't had any contact since. She tried to get news about him from other people, but no one had been able to shed light on the subject. She'd heard, of course, about Klaus's father: he'd been nearly blinded. It was a topic of discussion in the city, but Johana hadn't heard the story directly. Everyone knew that Klaus had been her fiancé; they avoided telling her what had happened.

But the days continued to pass and the country had changed. Johana was the lover of Ivor, the young officer. And Ivor punctually delivered Catharina's medication.

Ivor had left their house a few hours earlier. On that night Johana had begun reading a book, while Catharina lay down in the bedroom. She heard a faint noise. It was the window. The next moment, two men entered her home. Xalak and Klaus.

2

The two men are eating in the kitchen. Johana gives Xalak everything he requests. Klaus still hasn't said a word. Johana doesn't cry.

She merely asks them not to make any noise; her mother, Catharina, is sleeping.

Klaus is seated, smoking. A photograph of Ivor on the small table beside him.

Johana is facing him. Xalak's upper body is exposed, he's only wearing pants. He has sores on his mouth. He won't stop talking and he's drooling a lot. Johana asks him, please, speak more softly, so as not to wake up her mother. It would upset her, Johana says, she's not well.

Klaus still hasn't said a word.

Xalak, in the middle of an uninterrupted speech, says: I'll take the other one—and then he looks toward the door to the bedroom where Johana's mother is. Johana looks at Klaus. Klaus remains seated.

Xalak undresses completely. Johana lowers her eyes. Xalak asks Klaus for his cigarette. He takes a single drag and hands it back. I'm going in there, says Xalak, and he walks toward the bedroom. Klaus remains in the same position and tells him: Lock the door from the inside.

Xalak enters Catharina's bedroom, where she's still asleep, and locks it from the inside; the sound of the key turning can be heard.

Johana is standing, staring at Klaus. She trembles. She's unable to move. She's trembling a lot, a strange, intimate shudder.

Chapter XIII

1

Ivor embraces Johana.

We'll catch them. They escaped from prison yesterday. There are two of them.

Catharina has been hospitalized. Catharina needs constant medical attention. Ivor took care of everything.

She's doing well, says Ivor. You'll be able to visit her in a few days.
Johana doesn't say anything, just listens.

There are two of them, they've probably already joined the guerrillas.
One of the guards helped them escape: he's going to be executed two days from now. And a prostitute. They're still deciding if they're going to execute her too, or use her for something else. She knew what she was doing. She knew that they were going to escape and she knew that if it happened she would be executed; she went along with it anyway. She deserves to be executed in a more respectful manner than the guard. He betrayed his post, she didn't.
She's a fat woman, said Ivor, with enormous breasts. A well-known prostitute here in the city. We don't understand how she mustered the courage to do this. I'm curious to speak with her, to try to understand. A woman like that should be on our side, not theirs.

Johana was standing still and just listening. It had been hours since she'd gone into a fit of madness, but Ivor had arranged for a nurse to stay with her for those first few days as a precaution.

After three weeks, however, the cost was no longer bearable. Ivor also quickly lost interest in Johana. She was insane!

Nevertheless, it was Ivor who, two months later, took care of the paperwork necessary to commit Johana to the same clinic as her mother. After that day, Ivor never saw Johana again.

2

Alof embraced Klaus. He was the one who'd arranged the escape.

On that night there was a celebration. The men of the resistance were happy; they drank, they ate. Klaus was well known and respected by the enemy. It was clear that only his family's influence had saved him from execution. His mother, even after the events that had left his father partially blind, never stopped sending requests for her son to be granted clemency. That he could remain in prison, just so long as they didn't kill him. There was talk of executing Klaus week in and week out, but nothing ever came of it. And now Klaus had escaped.

Alof hadn't asked Klaus a single question about his time in prison. It wasn't the right time, and the right time would probably never come. Klaus had changed, Alof had noticed that much.

Xalak ate and drank at Klaus's side. Xalak never stopped drinking. Every now and then, Xalak, his lips covered in small sores, would let out a roar or sing the chorus of some popular song. Klaus remained silent and ate very little. When the meal ended, Xalak started to dance; some of the men clapped their hands and sang, encouraging him. Xalak, euphoric and naked from the waist up, as always, continued to dance. An animal, with his enormous scar.

A few hours passed and everyone was already asleep. Xalak was still awake and doing something absolutely irrational: he was yanking grass from the ground with his hands. Klaus went over to him. He said:

I never forgot—and then he pulled out a knife.

Xalak immediately grabbed the knife that he kept in his pants. Klaus threw himself on Xalak and ran the blade through his stomach. Xalak was able to regain his feet, he was a fighter after all, and responded with a thrust that brought his knife close to Klaus's face. They were face-to-face, Xalak bleeding but still strong, holding his knife at the ready, prepared to fight. Klaus was two meters away from him.

Suddenly there was a noise. It was Alof: he had sunk his knife into Xalak's neck. Xalak fell. He was still alive.

Go away, said Klaus. Leave me here alone.

Alof went off. He could still hear Klaus saying something to Xalak, who could no longer react:

I never forgot . . . Alof heard him say.

Klaus and Alof are seated together. The sun hasn't risen yet. They'd buried Xalak a few minutes earlier. Alof is smoking.

Neither of them said a word. They'd buried Xalak without exchanging a single word. Alof offered Klaus a cigarette. Klaus smoked a little. He had a blade in his hand. He coughed.

Let's try to get some sleep, said Alof, but neither of them moved.

Chapter XIV

1

A strong gale doesn't alter the shape of the night. The country seemed like it was divided into thousands of men: each man with his own language and his own death. There's no way to be trivial during wartime: all you can do is fantasize, or think about your own body, burnt black.

There was a personal death out there for Klaus, and he was searching for it. In commerce and death you should keep secrets to yourself: business deals and suicides aren't enacted with advance notice and processions in the street.

Klaus felt that he had entered a most personal night, a night that shared his name. It wasn't a universal night; not all living men had firmly planted the physical aspect of their being in this substance. The sensation that objects, and the earth, are losing their inner light, as if every single thing had its own grate, out of which all the light, not water, was draining, for light flows like water.

Klaus had a dagger; he raised it. It wasn't that night was issuing onto the blade, it was the blade itself which had lost its light. We don't have a soul, we have a grate, and Klaus smiled. And what if the ridiculous, ragged substances are the essential ones? Klaus asked himself.

He walked past the infirmary. He tried to get a good look inside it. At night the tools that cure have the same shape as the tools that kill. Only when you get up close can you tell whether a certain blade belongs to the benevolent realm of objects, if such a thing actually exists. The technique and the shape of each thing aren't elements with which you can calmly make friends. A blade contains all the malice of its velocity. It's all a question of velocity, of acceleration. A benevolent blade, if it strikes with speed, will cause damage to the body.

Klaus understood this phenomenon well. He didn't know how to calculate the average velocity of kindness and the average velocity of strength, and he couldn't explain the precise difference in rhythm between a blade that wants to stay in the body and a blade that doesn't. It gets all mixed up, and it gets even more mixed up during wartime.

At certain moments there is an intense traffic in blades and bodies, but afterwards the commotion suddenly disappears.

Klaus had already seen too many corpses. From time to time he thinks of those docile bodies as postage stamps affixed to the earth. And the ground is the proper place for those stamps. It always left an impression on him whenever he saw corpses hanging up high; he always closed his eyes in front of hanging victims, because corpses are a substance that is violated when left up in the air; corpses are the natural stamps that violent cities leave behind. The corpse is condemned to the earth. The earth is condemned to the corpse.

A stone that Klaus spotted became, at that instant, quite important. Stones are abandoned by men more often than plants or animals. The stupidest substance in the world—or, at final count, the most intelligent—is that which pretends to not need men.

That stupid, incompetent stone, thought Klaus. An incompetent stone, repeated Klaus. What would an incompetent stone be, what did it signify? A neutral, stupid thing, something that neither kills nor saves: there lies grave incompetence. But Klaus bent over and picked up the stone.

All of a sudden, Klaus perceived what appeared to be an intrusive clarity into his personal night, but no. It was a sound. It was the sound of Alof playing. In the middle of that mass of blackness. Does music contain light? Klaus asked himself. Not an electric light, not the light of machines, but an organic light, like with certain animals that give off light from their backsides: fireflies, and certain fish. Does music contain an organic light? It's that music is clearer at night, everyone notices this. Or else forms, when visible, diminish the clarity of the music. A struggle between solid shapes and the airy shapes of sound.

Klaus can feel his personal stone in his personal hand. On this night, the world is not collective. He doesn't feel any connection to the other men who belong to the resistance; he doesn't kill them, that's all. He doesn't want to kill them, that's it.

There are no hot flowers, thought Klaus, unless you piss on them. Klaus smiled. He had unbuttoned his pants; he was urinating on flowers that he didn't recognize, because within his personal night, a flower is just something that's taller than the ground. But they weren't flowers, they couldn't be flowers, flowers don't exist. And if they do exist, they're now hot flowers, at least for a minute or so, hot with Klaus's urine. He stupidly imagined a contest: the guerrillas, lined up side by side, urinating on the flowers. The man with the hottest urine would get to choose the woman he wanted. Johana's image appeared in his head, but Klaus immediately took a deep breath and forced himself to look down at his personal, incompetent stone. This rock would only serve to kill the sick and the elderly. Or children. It's an incompetent weapon, all techniques are incompetent during wartime if they fail to kill robust enemies with a certain efficiency and speed.

Klaus felt feverish. His personal fever had arrived. There were no doctors out there, but fever conceals itself better at night: you forget about it more easily.

But the fever grew and Klaus's head and thoughts were slowly redirected toward this sensation: he had a fever. He'd felt something ever since that morning, but during the day his body had been preoccupied with action, with saving itself. Fevers diminish when you're facing death.

But now his fever was growing. It seemed like the fever was jealous of that which his head had decided: the personal fever jealous of Klaus's personal decisions. The fever told him: There are things you can decide to introduce into the world, but there are still other things that don't belong to you. Fever appears, and you're the one that has it. A petty little fever emerges against your strong, personal will.

Klaus felt weak, not so much because of the physical effects of the fever, but because of what it represented at that moment. If a man is so free that he can decide to kill himself, how is it that, all of a sudden, that metallic temperature—that's what it is, a metallic temperature—can just come into being, right inside his very body? Does it come from inside or outside, that placid metal, that fever? To be able to grab a hold of the fever the way he grabs a hold of the stone; but no, the fever is not his.

Klaus thinks of the fever as a collective occurrence: If I can't control it, it doesn't belong to me, it's collective. Maybe it belongs to this region of the forest, or perhaps it belongs to the resistance, to the guerrillas as a whole. And Klaus can't help but feel a strong sense of disgust when he thinks about his companions in the resistance. He might be willing to die for them, but it disgusted him to think that he could catch an illness because of his proximity to them.

The other men were sleeping. Klaus had stopped listening to Alof play. But no: these things were only images that occupied the middle space between the body and everything else. But everything else carried on: Alof was still playing, perhaps he had never stopped, but to Klaus's personal mind the last few minutes had existed within the silence of everything else. And what is that everything else? Everything else is that which can die beside me. Anything that can die beside me is not me.

But it's not just an animal or a loved one that can die beside you (and thus "that" which dies is not you), there are also parts of your body that can die beside you and which, therefore, are not things that belong to you, even though they are personal to you. They can amputate your arm, and you can watch your arm die beside you: your arm can die beside you and therefore it can be your "everything else," and you still go on. And if there are things that you think are yours, like your arm, and they turn out to be the everything else of the world, that upon which, if necessary, you can spit, what are you to make of what remains? And what does remain? You can't spit in your own face, and this at least allows you to say that you have a personal face. But the world would be an even more precise place if a man could spit in his own face.

Klaus tried to vomit. He wasn't ill, but he thought about the act, and then, at the last minute, thought about stopping, so that the filth remained in an intermediate place. He held on to the vomit, pressing his lips together. The way he pressed them together in his first kisses, Klaus recalled. As if we were holding in something important.

But Klaus's head was a thing rendered barefoot. He didn't know how to explain the sensation, but it was an uncomfortable one: his head was barefoot.

Without protection. It touched the external world directly and the external world has cracks and edges that can cut you open. My head is barefoot, mumbled Klaus.

The thoughts inside of Klaus seemed like tools. The way a hammer has its own function. Thinking was the highest of functions: a profoundly personal function, a profoundly personal hammer, a hidden hammer.

Klaus sniffed himself. Thinking was something that existed in a place that was located opposite the place where smells are sensed. With great speed, Klaus crossed over from what he had been thinking to the smell of his own body. A smell is something external, it is the outer limit of the body; if it's a thought, thought Klaus, then a smell is the outermost thought of our body, something that is almost as external to us as a hat: our smell. While thoughts are protected by a series of thick layers, smell isn't.

But thoughts can't move vertically, thought Klaus, thoughts only move horizontally: they move forward the way a machine does, like train cars, but they don't jump into the air. They don't bump into stars, if they bump into anything it's the tree in front of them.

When you act, you forget about this internal movement, this internal commotion. As if all your thoughts are suddenly dissolved into one uniform substance. So, if everything is uniform here on the inside, we can take action out there on the outside; and, if necessary, act with precision, in a detailed manner, with great variety. If necessary, you can pick up a needle, and it's even easy; you have to dissolve your thoughts completely into nothingness, then pick up the needle with two fingers and make the smallest movement you can, a watchmaker's movement. Act with attention to detail in order not to think about big things.

Chapter XV

1

Don't clean the angels because the angels haven't yet begun to get dirty.

Of course they've begun, someone else said. We just haven't started to clean them, which is completely different. But no one remains clean; the war's been going on for too long.

The man smiled.

Now when we talk about filthiness, we laugh, he said. Because the only hygiene that matters to us is that which we need to survive. And to survive we do whatever is necessary, except for starting to clean.

No one is going to be saved that way. We perfect certain gestures, the way we do at work. And there's one thing we perfect before all else, though I'm not sure if it can be called a gesture, and that something is survival. It's not so much a gesture as a plan, a system of gestures: survive, survive, survive.

The day is divided into various moments, the way a square, drawn in pencil on paper, can be divided up into smaller and smaller squares. And in each square, the same objective. And that merely means that no separation has occurred: while we are alive, one day is like all the others. That's it. Survive. Continue to want to be alive.

The head was dislocated to the present. We have thoughts that occur in tandem with the moment we're in: neither in front of it nor behind. A daily head.

Shoes are very important, because they're the things that keep the intestines intact. The first time I heard this statement I thought it was absurd, but little by little I'm starting to understand it. If you have good shoes, your intestines will function just fine. It's absurd, but shoes are indispensable for fleeing and shitting. That's right. You heard well. Intestines aren't some second-class organ when what you want is to survive.

When people die, they all fall down to the same level. A plane, a bird, angels, a tall man, a dwarf. Have you ever noticed this? It would be interesting if tall men, when they fell, remained a few centimeters above the ground, suspended in the air by the few extra centimeters they have. But that doesn't happen. They all end up lying down, their full stature completely on the ground, like a towel. It's stupid. This fact renders the dimension of height insignificant.

But, if height is a secondary matter for a corpse, it isn't for an undertaker. And this is relevant. Economically relevant. The relatives of dwarves save money on wood, a cynical man once said to Klaus, and furthermore they can be doubly compassionate, because of the death and the corpse's tiny stature. Those are two advantages. Not everyone can argue the uses of compassion, a feeling that looks good on anyone's face. It makes faces more beautiful: a beautiful face, full of compassion.

No one can escape economic logic. Gains, losses, profit. Your coin might be strange—it might be your body, for example—but it's a coin, an instrument of commerce.

2

Klaus's hands are in his pockets. What a strange gesture, to hide his hands in his pockets. Hands and eyes are the foundation of war: without hands it's impossible to hate; you hate through your fingertips, as if your fingers were the sole, habitual conduit for a certain evil chemical substance. Putting your hands in your pockets is a process by which you tame your hatred, a slow process when compared to that much more powerful method that is the amputation of your arms. But only by putting their hands in their pockets do men grow calm.

With his hands in his pockets, a man understands that he is not God. He no longer reaches for things. If you touch the world with your head, you'll obtain, from this touch, secondary feelings, sensations of minimal intensity distanced from those to which your hands have accustomed you. Your hands make you more intense. How obscene—yes, that very thing—how obscene is the man who, during wartime, even during a pause in the action, provocatively puts his hands in his pockets. To admit that you are not God while a war's on is a courageous act and, as strange as it may seem, the only divine act. Only cowards pretend that they're God.

But for a few moments Klaus's existence is deprived of its intelligent organs: the hands, those highest organs of reason. Organs specialized in that primary instinct to survive: the primary instinct and the last instinct that a body will ever give up. With his hands in his pockets, Klaus can't avoid looking like an imbecile, a man who doesn't think.

And of course, putting your hands in your pockets makes emotion build up in the rest of your body. As if the fingers were secretly uncorking something. With your hands in your pockets you feel more, think less.

But Klaus's eyes had already seen bodies in enormous blue plastic bags. There is no wood, no matter how well-wrought, for covering up bodies that friends want to make disappear. Because consider this: enemies wish to exhibit their opponents' corpses, but friends who always wanted those bodies close to them in life now make them disappear into blue plastic bags with the utmost speed. And thus they quickly bury them. Klaus had already added a few of those black fruits to the ground, incubating them from top to bottom like some overzealous farmer who insists on demonstrating that his orders come from a point of verticality, not from the depths.

Inside a person's own clothes, hands take a break from touching one's lover or holding a murderous blade. Hands are organs susceptible to emotional inundation. Hands have more than just tactile feelings, they have more complex feelings too, like great sadness. To presume that there are elements of the body that neither suffer nor get angry, that merely watch, seems like an obvious mistake of that certain analytic body part which views each little bit of the body as a lone madman, with its own world. In an attempt to extract only the emotions from the body, there isn't a single organ you can remove and still keep the organism alive. You'll only extract the emotions when you eliminate the organism in its entirety. The last surviving cell still feels, and probably thinks too. But clearly the body isn't a Western object. Clearly the body wasn't invented in the West, even though people in the West may think so. (They invented everything: machines, ideas, language, why not the body as well?) But Klaus's body, with its hands in its pockets, was not a Western body. It was the body of a man.

For example: when a man engages in body-to-body combat with another, that man's entire organism becomes a mere fragment of his hands. Concerning a man who's had both arms amputated, you'd never say: he engaged in body-to-body combat. A man with no arms does not use his body to engage in combat.

And having your hands in your pockets is a transitory state between amputation and ferocious combat. It's a gesture of pacific violence, you could say.

With his hands in his pockets, Klaus had evaporated from the external world: he was thinking. He recalled the women who, in his youth, had fallen into his bed one after another. He recalled this sequence as an ensemble of aroused verbal clamor that varied from one woman to the next. The sounds that those women made in the act of making love: aroused verbal clamor. Klaus laughed at this formulation of his.

Because a verbal clamor was, in fact, a strange phenomenon. A formless clamor leads you immediately to the world of animals, a grotesque world, a world of that deficiency that is unable to express itself; and combining the verbal with this deformity yields a sense of strangeness. The verbal aspect of a speech, the verbal aspect of the law, the verbal aspect that is present even in a poem: since that world is human, and even more than human: of humans. It belongs to various man-things that are joined together. And thus the reason that fornication is so attractive and startling: it's the coming together of two worlds: the world of noises and the world of words, the world of Man and the world of animals, of nature, incomprehensible and raw, and yet still of Man, who attempts to understand. Klaus recalled his efforts to decipher the "verbal noises" of his lovers. What did they signify? Where was joy within these sounds?

Klaus, however, had always thought that it was easier to feign the human side of a sound—the verbal part—than the animal side of a sound—those deformed noises. In love, or more precisely, in fornication, Klaus had noticed that there clearly existed a sound with two faces—an animal face and a human face, and the only true face was the animalistic one.

To be revealed more fully during important moments by a language that doesn't exclusively belong to us, and which has belonged, for millions of years, to nature; such a fact seemed strange to Klaus, a man who, before the war, had always lived close to books. Could it be possible that the sound of a sentence is further removed from the human than the sound of wind rustling through things, through trees, or the sound of water? What is the meaning of the sounds of nature? Klaus had always wanted to know, but had never come to any conclusions. If I'm receiving these phrases, I should give some back, he thought. But are there phrases within the noises that nature makes? Or are natural sounds simply on the level of individual words, like how infants begin to acquire verbal language? The truth is that the dialogue had been cut off, and Klaus wasn't happy about that. He didn't understand the natural things that surrounded him and he knew that they didn't understand him either. And if books had been the barrier during peacetime—by being attracted to literature he had distanced himself from those sounds that he called primitive, those sounds that come from far away, from the external world, when you open a window—if it had been books during peacetime, during wartime it was the machines—in this case small machines, which were weapons—that had distanced him from nature. Because the clamor of bullets, of grenades . . . nothing in those deformed sounds had even the tiniest verbal vestige: this sound clearly wasn't human. But what really perplexed him was that the sound also wasn't natural. It wasn't an organic sound. Neither raw organic, nor intelligent organic, nor intellectually human organic. What sounds were they, then—the sound of a bullet, of a trigger being pulled back, of a grenade? That of a certain black sound—he was unable to come up with a better definition—a black sound that emanated from places where a bomb had exploded a few seconds earlier—what were those sounds?

Black sounds, sounds that were precisely black, as if there existed such things as thick water, compact water, inorganic water, water that makes noises that inexplicably call to mind body fragments. This, then, was the sound that existed after a bomb exploded: the sound of black water at high temperatures, black, thick water, which called to mind human body parts.

But what was the sound that emanated from machines, if it was neither the deformed sound of nature, nor a sentence? And if, whether up close or at a distance, it didn't resemble the animal/man mixture of lovers' moans that Klaus remembered? Could these sounds be, then, what some have termed over the course of History mystical sounds, sounds that are neither of men nor of the earth?

Because the sound of a bullet is not a sound of man, Klaus was sure about that. Because a man is unable to repeat the same intelligent sound or the same sentence twice, whereas those sounds were exact repetitions, repeated mechanically.

What frightened Klaus the most was this infallible mimicry. The fact that a weapon was, given the same conditions each time, able to repeat precisely the same sound with two different bullets. It was this possibility that frightened him and made him fear the third language more than the others, because the possibility of exact copies, of perfect repetition, was an obvious suspension of the customary conception of time, the time with which humans and nature are familiar: time that moves forward, that changes and alters things. And the machine, that small machine, as it repeated, stopped time; and as it demonstrated a copy of its previous "phrase," it demonstrated autonomy from the world: a temporal autonomy, a time that belonged not to this world, but autonomous time, which revealed a perfect power. A power that neither nature nor men—nature's most intelligent part—had achieved.

Klaus felt that within that sound, repeated thousands of times, there was the beginning of a power that would shortly conquer the earth. A power that would definitively stifle the "verbal noises" that his lovers had lodged in his corporeal memory.

Neither the sound of quotes from books, nor the sound of natural things knocking against other natural things, nor these two sounds mixed together in the physical act of lovemaking: Klaus's head was now fascinated by the sound, the nearly stupid, nearly History-less sound of bullets and bombs. The sound that proclaimed a new God.

Chapter XVI

1

Johana was in the same insane asylum as Catharina, her mother. Catharina was going to die in a few days, the doctor had told Johana. Johana had smiled.

Although Johana had been deprived of her wits, she still insisted on taking care of her mother, Catharina, as she had for the last fifteen years. But when Dr. Fluber told her that her mother had just died in a room on the third floor, Johana, lying on her own bed, again gave a smile which didn't fail to disturb those present.

During the last months of her life, Catharina wouldn't stop talking about an extremely skinny man with an enormous scar on his face who had fallen in love with her. No one aside from Johana could have known that her description corresponded to Xalak, the brutal man who had appeared that night, and who'd escaped from prison along with Klaus.

Even though Johana had lost control of her reason, she had never forgotten that night, and had understood very well what that skinny man with the enormous scar on his face had done to her mother. Johana, however, never attempted to contradict Catharina's story. She listened to her talk about this skinny man who had fallen in love with her, and sometimes she even agreed with her mother's mad ravings, saying: He really liked you.

You might think that Xalak's brutal actions that night would have tarnished whatever life remained for the elderly Catharina, but that isn't what happened. If Johana had been completely lucid when she observed her mother, she would have concluded that Catharina had never been as happy as she was during those final months when she repeated, endlessly, the story about the very skinny man with a scar on his face who had fallen in love with her one night.

Perhaps the smile on Johana's face, on the face of the sick woman that Johana had become, perhaps that smile, at the time of the news that her mother had just died, has its origins in what the doctor told her next:

I know suffering, Johana, and she died well.

It was then, at that moment, that Johana smiled that broad smile, as if she had a secret.

2

Herthe, meanwhile, had remarried. And she'd married a rich man: Leo Vast, the owner of two of the five biggest factories in the region. Leo Vast was fifty-three years old, Herthe was thirty-one. Through this marriage, Herthe had become a millionaire. Herthe Leo Vast.

Herthe Leo Vast liked to wear her fingernails long because it had always seemed to her an aristocratic touch. Happy, well-groomed fingernails infected the whole body, that was Herthe's philosophy in regard to those corporeal extremities. She was also meticulous about her toenails, and for that reason felt that her body was balanced: the two extremities, the two places where the body begins—the fingernails and toenails—received her dedicated attention. Because Herthe Leo Vast liked to think that that was where the body began: the nails. And it wasn't by chance that, as she'd been told, the nails were the last things to stop growing on a dead body. A precise circle.

Herthe, however, had never seen a corpse. Given that corpses were, during those times, what her husband Leo Vast called "articles of wide circulation," the fact that Herthe had never crossed paths with one—excepting the event that had recently transpired—revealed her aristocratic sensibility, which only chose and attended to that which was rare, and that to which ordinary people didn't have easy access. It was Leo Vast who said these things. Leo Vast further said, laughing: And if there's anything that ordinary people have easy access to these days, it's corpses. With detached irony and self-congratulatory black humor, Leo Vast said: Fortunately, that "organically immobile" and, what's worse, "organically useless and inefficient" article—the corpse—circulated more widely among those people of few resources than among the people with whom he had contact. Fortunately, people only die on the lower floors, he said, almost without any malice, Leo Vast, saying it merely for the pleasure he took in shocking people and, perhaps, saying aloud that which had popped into the heads of many other people, and which sometimes popped into his head too, the head of a benevolent man—which is what he considered himself to be.

I'm not out to demonstrate a pleasant fact, he said, I'm demonstrating a mere fact. I'll go so far as to say that it's a wicked fact, a negative fact for a society that wishes to be just, for justice will begin with equality of access to life and equality of access to death, or, in this case, equality of ease with which death arrives to a given body. It's clear that they have so many children, said Leo Vast, always in the same tone of voice, they have so many children that it is, in some way, a natural compensation from the other side, this ease with which they die. We could say that war is an instrument for maintaining a more-or-less balanced proportion of poor people to rich people, he said. After a prolonged period of peace, in which poor people procreate at a rate four to five times faster than the rich, who are stingy even in the distribution of their genes, let's say that after a period in which the structure of the world allows the poor to brutishly increase their hordes a war soon commences, no one knows where it comes from, in order to reinstate a quantitatively tolerable ratio between the common people and the elites. It's just that, despite everything, money has its limits in terms of physical force, and if the adversary were to keep multiplying, the struggle could take an irreversible turn that would lead to our defeat. And may the poor and the widows forgive me, said Leo Vast, amused, but nobody, nobody at all, likes to lose. Not even the rich.

Meanwhile, as was the general desire, Herthe became pregnant, and thus one day Leo Vast was interrupted in the middle of an important activity to be informed that his most excellent wife had entered the hospital, and was expected to give birth at any moment. Leo Vast, acting in a manner befitting this exceptional moment, excused himself, scheduled a new meeting for the following day, and left, with haste, for the hospital, where in just a few hours, or perhaps minutes, the first child of Leo Vast and his young wife, Herthe Leo Vast, would make its first appearance in this world.

But Leo Vast left his house worried: rumors were floating about that the war could be coming to an end. The afternoon newspaper had yet to arrive.

Chapter XVII

1

When Leo Vast arrived at the hospital, he immediately entered a room where Herthe's mother was nervously pushing Clako's wheelchair from one side to the other.

Well? asked Leo Vast.

Almost there, replied Herthe's mother.

A child who shall enter the next century, said Leo Vast, almost euphorically. This is going to be a great century, a great century! he repeated, as he ceaselessly, anxiously paced the floor.

No one can describe the philosophy of a country better than its army, the way in which its nationals behave at the moment of victory. A nation's philosophy should be assessed based on the everyday cruelties of its most ordinary people. The man who buries bodies under his garden, and the eccentric saint who's incapable of saying even a single bad word about his neighbor, are false instances that distort the reflection of a given nation's evil. What poor people do, when they're gathered in great numbers and are momentarily in power—Leo Vast was wont to say—it is this that allows you to characterize a country. Personalities don't count. All scientific studies utilize, as a matter of course, large numbers, which allow them to draw general conclusions.

At that time, Clako was a physically neutralized young man, though accepted and respected in the city. Invalid in terms of movement and language, in need of someone else to move him around, feed him, and lay him down, he nevertheless did not have that illness we call lack of money.

Clako was always impeccably dressed. Herthe, his sister, never neglected a single detail. Sometimes she joked with him in the presence of their mother, saying: Today's the day you're going to snatch up a bride, my dear brother.

Such an insinuation wasn't completely off the mark. Herthe and her mother were looking for a bride for Clako, someone who could take care of him. A bride who would push his wheelchair, push food into his mouth, and love him.

It would have to be an ambitious person, someone who would see in her engagement to Clako what entering Leo Vast's family represented. However, it would have to be someone with some financial self-respect. At least half-poor and not completely poor, said Leo Vast, so that a certain minimum financial level is maintained in this amorous transaction. It was, therefore, with these conditions in mind that Herthe searched for a bride for her brother. As for Clako, he couldn't move, couldn't communicate; he listened. And just listening means just accepting. In September of this year Clako became engaged to Emilia, a young woman with the desired characteristics. And in December they wed.

Pieces of information can be heard, but to act in away that's capable of being heard is practically despicable. Because to act is to be close to things, and to hear is to be far removed from them. Someone who merely hears something will never be thought of as intruding upon the world, nature will not feel threatened. The person who hears can accumulate information, but this accumulation will never challenge nature. Nature can successfully defend itself against Man's intelligence, reason, and memory; all of these intellectual qualities pertain exclusively to the world of the city, and that which threatens nature are actions: the moments when humans stop listening, even to the language of a speech, and begin to want to speak with their tactile sense, the only sense that can alter the nature of things. If men, maintaining their intelligence undefiled, were immobile beings, incapable of any movement at all, they would be less powerful at this point in time than a single square meter of unpredictable soil. They could possess a level of perfection in abstract thought, mathematics, and logic, but they would always be a second-class species in comparison with others: with those in possession of movement. Any mangy mutt could piss on the legs of a highly intelligent and yet immobile man. If, all of a sudden, in a completely absurd hypothetical situation, all human beings suffered accidents like Clako's, the human species would rapidly disappear within a generation. Thus, within a single generation, mathematics and logic would disappear from the world. And geometry. And literature.

If mathematics is so divine and universal, how can we explain the fact that the elimination of a single species—Man—out of the billions of living species would completely wipe numerical logic from the face of the earth? If we're going use the term "divine" to describe that which is widespread among nature's creatures, then the divine is movement and the ability to procreate; mathematics is merely the specialty of a small minority.

Clako had retained that which was exclusive to man, but had lost that which was exclusive to those beings touched by the divine. And this was the strange, unbalanced state in which he found himself. His intelligence and his will were intact, but he lacked words and, above all, movements capable of interfering with the History of the world, or even merely in his own History. And thus, in a few short years, he began to view everything with serene acceptance. More than simply resigned, Clako was happy in his marriage. Happy is the right word.

Meanwhile, in the maternity ward, events were transpiring at the desired speed. At first, crying was heard from far off, and then, minutes later, a door opened and a nurse emerged from behind it carrying a baby.

It's a boy, Mr. Leo Vast. A boy.

Chapter XVIII

1

Newspapers, by means of the news they contain, produce a constant clamor. A clamor that is maintained so long as someone is reading them. But the following occurs with the news: individual suffering and private joys disappear, and everything becomes collective property: newspaper as universal theory of the nonexistence of the individual. The person-event only exists if there is a person-spectator. Absolute, true privacy, pure individuality, aren't instances as such, they're non-instances, that is, literally: individuality (which has zero spectators) does not occur. You could almost assert that a private, individual existence is nothing more than an individual invention. How do you prove the existence of purely private moments, witnessed only by your own, private consciousness? We can't prove it, we can only believe it. I believe that the other exists as an individual. I believe: belief. I don't know: it isn't knowledge. But I know about myself: I know about my private moments, and I merely hope that others believe in the existence of such things. Every part of our lives that is witnessed by someone follows the newspaper's model: they see what's occurring or what's occurred. And that alone exists within History. And that which remains outside of History is the individual.

After a day at the hospital with his newborn baby—named Henry Leo Vast—Leo Vast, the father, finally unfolded the newspaper in late afternoon. And it was to his great surprise that he read, in letters covering the entire front page:
THE WAR HAS ENDED!
And at this moment he couldn't help but feel afraid.
Intensely afraid.

2

A thought becomes a part of the landscape when it isn't transformed into an act. And the landscape is something you step on or look at.

All processes of reasoning are unfinished, to breathe is to interrupt the trajectory of a logical process that could be mathematical/numerical in nature. The private narrative in your head interrupted by the need for oxygen: measly substances in the atmosphere—chemically formulated, but deprived of the divine formula—rise and fall throughout your body, as if suffused with meaning.

The only indispensible precondition for thought is that you aren't at that moment threatened with death and survival isn't a matter of some urgency. That much seems obvious. Thinking means you can put off surviving until later. Mental exercises concerning the future are not performed by two animals engaged in body-to-body combat. The extraordinarily close proximity of your body to another hostile organism impedes the progress of ideas. Thus, iron is a substance that logic cannot tolerate, while on the other hand, logical reasoning is immaterial, volatile, like substances in flight.

There are no metaphors in mathematics. Mathematics is simple thought, without replicas or symmetries. There are no two numbers that are parallel to each other, as with two straight lines. Numbers are individual and absolute.

It's not useful to dwell too much on what's occurred. The same force that previously threw the country into war, that same force now imposes its end. And the war stopped. In almost the same abrupt, surprising manner in which it began. That's it.

Men had been drinking water apprehensively. But now they drink it with the luxury of being unafraid. Domestic animals have reappeared. Even animals become more commonplace when the calm emerges. Indeed, Herthe Leo Vast had a dog she said was acting rabid. It would shriek, urinate in fits and starts, and sometimes come close to biting its owners. On the day that Herthe became a mother, she called Leo Vast over to her side within an hour of giving birth and told him:

I want you to kill the dog. Let's make a fresh start. We have to clean the ground.

Leo Vast returned home and, after reading the newspaper attentively, grabbed the dog by its collar and dragged it into the yard. He called a servant over.

Congratulations, sir, the man said to him.

For what? he replied curtly.

For the birth of your child, he said.

Yes, it's a boy, said Leo Vast, handing the dog to the servant.

Shoot it, he said. Then destroy the doghouse.

And he added:

Things are changing.

Leo Vast was already attentively reading the second edition of the newspaper, which had come out late in the afternoon with details of new developments, when, startled, he almost jumped out of his seat: a gunshot!

He recomposed himself. It came from the yard, it was his servant.

He felt relieved; the day continued. Nothing significant has changed, he thought.

He got up to give the servant some suggestions about where the dog could be buried.

Noise, noise, muttered Leo Vast.

Chapter XIX

1

Democracy assumes its place in a country like a piece of rubber that slowly melts until it completely fills the dimensions of its container. But democracy is the establishment of mutual cowardice, and such a system is never dissevered from a powerful will, from an original intention; on the contrary, it results from the melted material. Democracy isn't a political system that's made of fundamental materials. It's fire that produces it; it's the excessive heat, the insufferable heat which produces the serene détente. And the fundamental material, the primary Power, will only be re-established after a prolonged period of cold. Democracy results from a group of men losing power. It's a global acquisition of weakness.

It was Leo Vast who exemplified this state at that moment. The rubber has melted, he muttered. They've melted the powerful material and now our feet are stuck in a spongy material. We don't know what's going to happen.

But Leo Vast's family withstood the changes comfortably. It was as if political change only affected the society's bottom tier, never reaching the higher levels. Money is democratic if necessary, and dictatorial if necessary. It's an elastic material *par excellence*. It obeys the laws that it imposes upon itself: thus is money.

2

Industrialist Leo Vast, his young wife, Herthe, his six-year-old son Henry, Herthe's brother Clako, immobilized in his wheelchair, with his young, beautiful wife, Emilia, at his side—the lot of them made up the inner structure of Leo Vast's family, one of the most powerful in the city. Herthe Leo Vast's mother had died two years earlier, and Herthe now took care of two children, as industrialist Leo Vast never tired of repeating: Henry himself, the pride of the family, and Clako, her brother. At times, Leo Vast was unable to hold back certain feelings of jealousy caused by all the attention Herthe paid to Clako—she was the one who, on certain days, even in the presence of Clako's wife, insisted on feeding him—and at certain moments the powerful man would insinuate that Clako and Emilia would perhaps be better off in their own house, and not his. Nevertheless, Herthe was unyielding:

He's my brother, he's not leaving my side.

Furthermore, he was now the only living member of her original family.

Clako, meanwhile, hadn't made any progress; although he hadn't gotten worse, he could only move a few fingers and wasn't able to speak or write. His situation was stable.

At times, Leo Vast was unable to hold back the thought that Clako was just another piece of furniture in his enormous house, except he was a piece of furniture that ate, that ended up costing more than normal furniture. He was like a piece of furniture that had come from Herthe's parents' house—his wife's parents—thus explaining her emotional connection to it. Without any malice, merely by way of the instinctive incontinence of his thoughts, Leo Vast would say to himself, that any object that made you remember relatives that were already gone should be thrown out, so that excessive melancholy doesn't take root in the house. Leo Vast didn't stop in time to keep himself from thinking that throwing Clako out with the trash would be as easy and as devoid of struggle or opposition as throwing a table or chair out the window. And he asked himself: A man who doesn't resist as he's being thrown out with the trash belongs to what living species? But suddenly Leo Vast stopped. Clako, immobilized before him in a wheelchair, had a look in his eyes that revealed nothing, save that he was a body that had been reduced to a single function: to wait for others to do things for him.

Among all the functions of man, the bullets had only left his body with the most passive of them, the weakest function, the one that expressed man's organic misery: waiting. And thus Leo Vast looked at that immobilized body in its wheelchair and felt something that he couldn't completely identify. He had an emotional connection to that body, which was strange in its way. He hadn't known Clako before the accident, not a drop of blood bound them together; it was a body that had never spoken to him, and what's more, it had never heard him; an inert, indifferent body, mere matter, and yet, Leo Vast felt something intense. When Clako was far away from him, he could think about him with indifference, but when he took time to observe Clako, he was moved. Leo Vast was sometimes even stirred by the conviction that there was a stronger emotional bond between him and Clako than between him and his wife. And that only his son, Henry, surpassed that handicapped body in terms of inspiring affection. Leo Vast liked to think clearly: if Clako were to die, he would suffer more than upon the eventual death of his wife. Herthe was a strong woman, she didn't need him. She could die, she could tread toward death alone, and she'd know how to defend herself. But not Clako.

Perhaps in this his competitive instinct was made visible, or even more than that: his animalistic instinct to fight. He had been trained to eliminate the strong and protect the weak. The weak, dependent on him, would work; the strong would steal from him. Regarding Herthe, this was somewhat how he felt: she was a strong woman, too strong, even for him. She was equipped to steal from him, and had the strength to do it. Thus, he loved her moderately and feared her greatly. While he stared at Clako, sitting there motionless, waiting for others, Leo Vast realized that if he wanted to he could spit in his face, and for that reason kissed him a few times. I'm kissing you because I can spit on you whenever I want.

Furthermore, Leo Vast was starting to feel old. He understood that he now had few years ahead of him. If he still wanted to like someone, he would have to hurry.

Chapter XX

1

Henry Leo Vast had grown up entirely during peacetime, and also in a democracy.

You were born the same day that the war ended, his parents told him repeatedly. You ended the war.

He was now twelve years old, and he was already a strong boy. One of the city's eminent heirs.

The mouth is the locus of the "first positive happiness," so a "psychology of lips" is essential if you're to understand liquids like milk or water. A certain author also mentions a "grammar of necessity": an organism is an object that desires. And thus the fundamental difference: other objects don't desire.

Across the space of an area, children habitually hide abominable things. A child hides a watch under the dirt in a small flowerpot. So that the plant will grow at a steady rate, she thinks. A watch buried in the dirt.

Certain children fall ill, but they're healed. To quote from the Book of Revelation: ". . . and the leaves of the tree were for the healing of the nations." The war began when certain nations in disagreement lost some of their leaves from the healing grove; in Autumn nations have more illnesses, and unhappiness assaults the population.

Certain beliefs, however, encourage strange behaviors. A prostitute places seeds in her shoes so that she'll crush them as she walks. It's believed that the elements of life will thus grow more readily.

Some indicators of peace: men gather together less, there are fewer groups. It's a fact: solitude increases in peaceful countries. We draw near to each other to protect ourselves. We come together out of selfishness.

Mouths are important in wartime, people are hungry; during periods of democracy, lips still retain their importance, but now they're busy with speech. Language is used more often in peacetime, let there be no doubt: in wartime there are no conversations, just information. Quick, brief sentences.

Laziness takes root. At times, Klaus is faced with something novel: sluggishness. But that's rare. Klaus works a lot. Klaus returned to the city a long time ago, and took up his place in the Klump family.

In the meantime, the economy had grown the way children grow. Certain numbers that used to be small are now large. Professions were created in order to organize the world. All space, every cubic meter, should be occupied by professions. And all time, as well: from the moment you wake until you go to sleep, better to be occupied by a profession. Every square meter occupied by some utility, every spare second as useful as farmland. Space for those who will work it, but also time for those who will work it. Because there are some people who will not work the time they're given.

Klaus wasn't one of them. Klaus took over the factories that had belonged to his father and in the first few months employed countless men. However, he quickly abandoned this impulse: you don't wind up with a lot of money when you have to pay a lot of people.

For a businessman, rust on powerful machines is more worrisome than an employee's hepatitis. It's obvious, you can't even measure those two things against each other on the scales. How much is rust on the machine worth? A hundred men with hepatitis? How do you make such calculations without brutality, but still with precision?

2

Klaus's father had died a few months before the end of the war. Nearly blind as a result of the shard of glass that his son had one day stabbed into his eye.

Klaus's mother had never spoken of "this": it was an occurrence that had not occurred. The war had been over for a long time, and Klaus was now a very well-respected man in the city: on top of being rich, he had also been a combatant, one of the most brilliant.

It was with obvious joy that Klaus's mother welcomed her son as, upon his return, he shortly assumed control of his father's business. At first he hesitated still, thinking that he might make a powerful entrance into politics. But a year after his return he was still firmly at his place in the family. His mother would tell him: The factories need a boss.

Klaus grabbed hold of the family business as he'd previously grabbed hold of weapons: calmly and coldly. He was alive, still had quite a few years ahead of him, his life had been hell, and there was nothing left but to press onward: to survive, to be as happy as possible, to mark the earth with our names. Our individual names.

The populace doesn't have a collective name. Nor do any two people have a collective name. There are always two different names for two different things, and two men are two different things. You can't mark a single piece of earth with two different names; if you do that, you'll start a war, or else a wedding.

There are exercises for practicing truth, like, for example, being afraid. Or being hungry. Then there are exercises for practicing lies: all groups are examples of this, and all businesses.

Being in love is another way of exercising truth.

Klaus was in charge of the family business for the first time. He wasn't afraid, wasn't hungry; nor was he in love. Every day was, thus, a new exercise in lying. He'd already made a real life for himself (he'd made it the way you construct a building, something material), and now he was entering the game: make more money or lose money. Nothing essential about it, but interesting lies are those that almost seem true. Klaus felt the need to transform that game into something fundamental. And he would carry on until the end. As he'd done before, in war and in prison. As a matter of fact, he almost couldn't see the difference between those three situations: it was necessary to win or at least not lose, and he was alone. That was it.

Alof, on the other hand, was a simple man. He reopened his music shop and took up music again. I stopped playing music in the middle of a note; years later I'm picking it up again at the exact same spot, and I'll go on from there. But of course that wasn't the case: he had forgotten a lot of the notes from before. It wasn't enough to start off at the point where he'd stopped playing music. He would have to go back further, reconstruct the beginning of the melody, call it back to mind. Only months or even years later would he then be at the spot where he'd left off. Or perhaps he would never return there.

And that's really what happened: Alof stopped playing. It's true that he kept his shop open for a few months, starting it back up with financial support from Klaus, but shortly thereafter he lost interest. He sold the shop and accepted a job in some old shop. However, he still paid back all the money Klaus had lent him. Klaus didn't want to take it, but Alof insisted.

We lead a different life now. You don't owe me anything and I don't owe you anything. It's good to keep precise accounts. You lent me two hundred, and I'm giving you two hundred back.

At the moment when the money was being returned to him, Klaus couldn't avoid the thought that, to be perfectly fair, Alof shouldn't pay him back the two hundred he'd borrowed, but instead a little more, since a year and a half had passed and the money had depreciated. But Klaus kept quiet. And accepted what Alof had given him back.

Chapter XXI

1

Henry Leo Vast was already sixteen years old and had inherited his sarcastic irony from his father, the first Leo Vast, who had passed away the summer before.

Herthe Leo Vast was now in charge of the business, but she was anxious to introduce Henry to the countless tasks that managing a small empire required. At the age of eighteen, her son would take over all responsibilities.

It was Sunday, the day that families went out for a stroll, and the most sought-after bachelor in the city, Klaus Klump, arm in arm with his mother, cordially bid hello to Alof and his wife, who was wearing a dress in particularly poor taste; Klaus didn't stop, however, for he had spotted, off in the distance, the procession of the family of Leo Vast.

Herthe Leo Vast, owner of the empire she had inherited from Leo Vast, and Klaus Klump, owner of the slightly more modest Klump family empire, walked toward each other with restrained gestures, but with evident smiles on their faces. Alongside Herthe Leo Vast was her son Henry Leo Vast, her brother Clako, and his pretty wife Emilia, who pushed the wheelchair. They all looked happy. Klaus Klump's mother, ever arm in arm with her son and already slightly senile, smiled at everyone.

They exchanged prolonged greetings. The families were about to make an important business deal which would be advantageous for both parties. The contract would be signed later that week. They joked around a bit, with young Henry proving to be the sharpest.

Meanwhile, less than a hundred meters from this incidental yet significant encounter, a prostitute, leaning against a wall, attempted to seduce customers.

They do it in broad daylight now, muttered Herthe Leo Vast, annoyed.

They all turned their heads and looked over at the woman. They fell silent. Her blatant short dress annoyed them. Even from that distance, the woman must have sensed she was being watched, and she lowered her head.

It'll be the end of this city, said Herthe Leo Vast for the second time.

Tomorrow, without fail, I'm going to present a formal protest to the president of the city council, added Klaus Klump, unable to contain his indignation.

Yes, they all agreed. Yes.

Notebooks of Gonçalo M. Tavares | 7